Haki the Shetland Pony

This is the story of Adam Cromarty and his
Shetland colt Haki. Haki was born on Adam's
father's croft, and was given to Adam for his own.
A strong sympathy grew up between them, and
Adam spent a lot of time and trouble on Haki's
training. But the day came when Adam was told
the pony must be sold, And sold he was – to a
circus. . .

KU-487-780

HAKI
the Shetland pony

KATHLEEN FIDLER

ILLUSTRATED BY VICTOR G. AMBRUS

KNIGHT BOOKS
Hodder & Stoughton

For Kathleen Helen McTaggart
Isobel Anne McTaggart
James Harold Goldie
with my love

My thanks are due to Mr John Smith and to his daughter
Miss Eva Smith of Berry, Scalloway, Shetland, for their
kind help

ISBN 0 340 16947 8

Text copyright © 1968 Kathleen A. Goldie
First published in 1968
by Lutterworth Press, London
This edition first published 1973
by Knight, the paperback division of Brockhampton Press (now Hodder
& Stoughton Children's Books), Salisbury Road, Leicester
Third impression 1976
Printed and bound in Great Britain
by Cox & Wyman Ltd,
London, Reading and Fakenham

This book is sold subject to the condition
that it shall not by way of trade or otherwise be
lent, re-sold, hired out or otherwise circulated
without the publisher's prior consent in any form of
binding or cover other than that in which this is
published and without a similar condition
including this condition being imposed
on the subsequent purchaser.

Contents

The colt is born

'Why are you taking your porridge so fast, laddie?'

Mrs Cromarty watched Adam gulping down a spoonful of porridge so hot that it brought tears to his eyes.

'Got to be at the school.' Adam almost choked on the words.

'Guid sakes! You've time enough yet. Have you no' finished your homework?'

'Aye, it's finished.'

'Then why are you turning your inside into a burning fiery furnace? Take more milk!' Mrs Cromarty poured a generous measure of milk into Adam's bowl. 'Now, if it's a game of football with Ian Sinclair and the other lads before the school starts you can just hold yourself back and take your breakfast quietly.'

Magnus Cromarty, Adam's father, watched Adam with amused eyes in which there was a hint of sympathy. At last Adam finished the porridge and the buttered barley scone that his mother made him eat. He snatched his school satchel from the hook behind the kitchen door.

'I'm off now!' he said and fled before his mother could find any other excuse to keep him back.

'Och, those lads and their football!' she cried as the door banged.

Mr Cromarty smiled a little. 'Maybe it's no' the football that's taken Adam so early to the school.'

'What then?'

'Hecla is due to have her foal any time now. You know we promised Adam that this foal should be his own. He'll be anxious to see if the foal's born yet.'

'He's never going up over the hillside before school! He'll be late!' Mrs Cromarty rushed to the door, flung it open and shouted 'Adam! Adam!'

'You can save your breath to cool your own porridge,' Magnus told her with a laugh. 'The lad'll be over the hill with the wind behind him now. He'll never hear you.'

'He's crazy about that pony,' Mrs Cromarty said. 'Every evening after his tea he's up the hill to take a look at Hecla. I wonder that he gets his homework done at all. But this is a new thing, rushing up after breakfast.'

Adam had doubled round the corner of the cottage and past the patchwork of his father's small fields around the Shetland croft. He sprinted past the barley field and the potato drills, past the hay field and the small pasture with its few cows, through the rough tussocky grass where the sheep moved lazily aside as he sped upwards. At last he reached the stony Hill of Berry beyond, gashed with the black peat banks and covered with stubbly heather. This was where the Shetland mare, Hecla, grazed. Adam paused and his eyes searched the hillside. No sign of Hecla anywhere, munching at the new green shoots of heather!

When her time was near, Hecla always sought out a sheltered nook to give birth to her foal, a place where she was sheltered from the easterly wind; where she could be hidden from other animals and human beings. All Shetland mares did this when their time came for them to bring out their young. Adam pursed his lips to whistle for Hecla, then stopped before the sound left his mouth. Hecla would want no one at this time. He must look for her quietly. He climbed higher still and stared over the moorland. School was forgotten! He remembered the old abandoned small quarry dug into the breast of the hill. He had seen Hecla nosing round there several times lately. He climbed above the quarry and came slowly and cautiously down to the lip of it. Hecla was there!

She was lying on her side, her flanks still heaving with the effort she had made. There, lying between her legs, was the newly born foal, weak and slumped together. Adam drew in his breath sharply. 'It's born! It's born!' he whispered to himself with fierce delight. 'It's born, and it's to be *my* pony!'

As he watched, Hecla stirred herself and lifted her head to look at her new-born child. She rolled a little, lifting her hind leg clear of the foal. Then she pulled herself round and nosed the little animal. Her tongue came out and she licked him gently, carefully, all over.

9

'It's a colt!' Adam said to himself in delight. 'A lovely chestnut colt!'

The little creature nuzzled closer to Hecla. He was no bigger than a medium-sized dog. His eyes were blind and would stay so for three or four days. Until he could see he would know his mother only by her smell. His nostrils flared wide as he drew in her scent. Both mother and new-born son rested and slept.

Adam watched them fascinated, forgetting the time. From away down in the valley came the sound of a vigorously rung handbell. The teacher was standing on the school steps summoning the pupils. Adam started guiltily. No matter how he ran now, he would be late, very late! Reluctantly he turned away from Hecla and her foal and began the long run down the hill to the small town of Scalloway. He reached the road, its banks starred with the late May primroses of the Shetland Isles. Past the outlying houses he ran, their gardens hedged by the flowering currant. All his life afterwards when Adam smelt the sharp aromatic scent of the currant it called to his mind this particular day.

'What shall I call the colt?' he kept asking himself. 'It must be a fine bold name.'

It was not till he reached the school door that he came down to earth. Miss Gourlay would have something to say because he was late. She would want to know the reason. Adam opened the classroom door as quietly as he could and slipped into his seat.

'What kept ye?' Ian Sinclair, his desk-mate,

whispered to him. Ian was Adam's particular friend and confidant. 'Was it Hecla?'

Adam nodded.

'Has she foaled?'

'Aye.'

'What is it?'

'A colt. A beauty!' Adam could not help saying with pride.

Ian knew the colt was to be Adam's. 'Man, you're in luck!' he whispered.

When the morning break came, Adam talked quietly with Ian in the playground.

'The colt was only just born, Ian. I watched Hecla lick him over. He hadn't even tried to stand and Hecla hadn't risen either. I think she'll be all right. It's not her first foal. She might be thirsty though. There's a little lochan not far from the quarry. I'll take her some water from there in the dinner break. She's sometimes been difficult about feeding her foals. There was one once that she left altogether and we had to feed it with a baby's bottle. She's more likely to refuse to feed him if she hasn't got water to drink herself.'

'How will you carry water from the lochan to Hecla?'

'I'll borrow a bucket from Mr Anderson, the caretaker.'

As soon as the bell rang for the close of the morning session Adam tore out of the classroom and sought out Mr Anderson to borrow his bucket.

Five minutes later Adam Cromarty was racing

up the hill for all he was worth with a red plastic bucket in his hand.

Panting hard, his breath tearing him like a knife, he reached the little lake and plunged his bucket into it. Then he sought out Hecla in her resting place inside the quarry. She was lying there with her colt beside her. He was no larger than a collie dog and had thin spindly legs that looked as if they would hardly support him.

'Hecla! Hecla!' Adam called in a gentle voice.

The Shetland mare tossed the long mane of thick straight hair that fell over her eyes and turned her head to look at Adam. She was small and neat, not more than thirty-eight inches high from the ground to the top of her shoulders. Adam advanced a little closer and halted. He had to be particularly careful not to alarm her. The little mare was suspicious of any living thing that moved towards them and was anxious to protect her foal.

'Hecla! Hecla!' Adam called softly. This time she recognized his voice. Adam was a friend. Adam went a few feet nearer and set down the red plastic bucket of water closer to her. Then he sat down to watch.

Hecla eyed the bucket for a few minutes and caught sight of the glint of water within it. This might be some trap, though. She turned her head to look at Adam again. He was sitting on a boulder, not attempting to come any nearer. Cautiously she approached within a foot or two of the bucket, the foal nosing after her. She stopped again and sniffed

suspiciously and looked all round her. Adam kept still as a post. Then she grew bolder and sniffed at the bucket. A moment later her nose was into the bucket and she was drinking thirstily. At last her thirst was slaked and she lifted her head from the bucket and looked at Adam.

'Hecla!' he said persuasively and held out his hand towards her. She came at his call and nuzzled at his arms and hands and poked her nose into his pocket.

'So you've not forgotten?' Adam whispered and felt in his pocket for the lump of sugar he had put there that morning. He held it out on the palm of his hand and she took it gently between her teeth. The foal missed her and whinnied nervously. She turned at once to him and stood between him and Adam.

'It's all right, lassie! I will not try to touch him yet. We'll wait for that,' Adam told her reassuringly. 'But one day that colt will come to me of himself.'

The foal found Hecla and pressed his head beneath her and sought for milk. At first she moved away impatiently. The foal followed her. It was as though he needed protection and comfort even more than food. To Hecla he turned blindly for these. At last she stood still, calm in her motherhood, while he sucked.

Adam drew a deep breath. There was no need to persuade Hecla to accept her foal this time; no need for bottle feeding.

14

'She's going to feed him. It's going to be all right,' Adam said to himself happily. 'Good lassie, Hecla! She's moving about now, too, and soon she'll go down to the lochan herself for water.'

Suddenly he remembered school. He snatched up the bucket and made off down the hill as fast as he could.

That afternoon he tried hard to concentrate, especially in Miss Gourlay's history lesson, and not let his thoughts wander to Hecla and the foal. Miss Gourlay was speaking of early Viking exploration of the western world and how Leif was the first European to discover the shores of America, long before the time of Christopher Columbus. The Shetlanders were proud of their descent from the Vikings. Suddenly Adam heard the word 'Hecla' and his eyes opened wide.

'The Norsemen put ashore two people, a man and a woman who were wonderful runners. They had to run through the country and explore it for two days and then come back to the ship on the second night with a report. Their names were Haki and Hecla. It is thought they might have been Shetlanders or Scots, but Haki and Hecla were the first people to explore America.'

'Hecla!' Ian whispered and pinched Adam.

'I know what I'm going to call that foal,' Adam whispered back. 'I'm going to call him *Haki*.'

'Haki!' he thought to himself. 'A fine name! It's just the name for the colt. Haki!'

2

Haki begins to learn

Every day Adam went whistling up the Hill of
Berry to look at Hecla and Haki as they roamed the
scathold, or common grazing land. On these moor-
lands the crofters have the right to graze a number
of ponies or sheep according to the size of their
small farms. The ponies range freely over the hill.
Even in winter they are never brought into stables
unless they show signs of illness. They are hardy
little animals who prefer the open hill ground and
thrive best on it. Their coats are thick and heavy
and shed the rain so that their skins never become
wet. In winter snow storms they find shelter behind
a wall or peatbank till the worst of the storm is past.
Sometimes, if the snow lies for any length of time,
the crofters bring the ponies down near their farms
so that they can feed hay to them. Even then the
ponies scrape with their feet at the snow till they
have uncovered the rough coarse grass beneath,
which they like better than hay.

It was late May when Haki was born. As Hecla
roamed over the hill Haki followed close at her side.
When the mare stopped to graze Haki sucked
hungrily at his mother. His legs grew strong and
supple as he gambolled about her. Whenever other
mares became too curious or a human being ap-

proached, Haki flew to Hecla. The taste of her warm sweet milk in his mouth gave him comfort and protection.

Adam was too wise in the ways of Shetland mares and colts to risk frightening the colt. He pretended to take no notice of him, but every day he brought a couple of lumps of sugar to Hecla. Always, as he drew near them, he whistled the same tune, then called to Hecla in a quiet voice. The mare twitched her ears when she heard him coming over the heather and lifted her head to watch for him. Haki ran to the side of Hecla furthest from Adam and dived under his mother for comfort. Adam always stopped a few paces away and called: 'Come, Hecla, Come!' and held out his hand with the sugar on the palm.

Hecla shook off Haki impatiently and came towards Adam, Haki striving desperately to suck from her. He hid beneath her as she took the sugar from Adam. Adam made no attempt to touch him at all. Day after day he went through the same routine till Haki got used to him. Then, one day, his patience was rewarded. Haki did not bolt beneath his mother at Adam's approach but stood his ground and looked at Adam.

'We're getting on!' Adam thought in triumph. He looked towards the little colt and called gently, 'Haki! Haki!' Haki lifted his head and looked at him again. The two eyed each other quietly and in that moment confidence was born in the colt and he knew Adam for a friend.

The next time Adam came up the hill he brought some extra sugar in his other pocket. When Hecla came forward to take her two lumps from Adam's outstretched hand Haki moved alongside her and did not hang back.

'Haki! Haki!' Adam spoke very softly and held out his left hand with the other two lumps of sugar towards Haki. At first Haki shied slightly, but when Adam made no further move towards him, he regained his confidence. Curiosity got the better of him. Keeping close to Hecla he moved towards the extended hand and sniffed. The sugar smelt good. He gave a rasping lick of his tongue and the sugar was in his mouth! He backed away quickly from Adam but Adam neither tried to touch him nor drew his hand back too quickly. The first move between them had been made and accepted. That was enough for a beginning.

Haki soon grew to expect his daily sugar from Adam. When Hecla raised her head expectantly as Adam came up the hill, Haki did the same. With her he came to Adam. Then, one day, as Haki munched at the sugar, Adam slowly brought up his hand and rubbed him between the ears. Haki flicked his ears in surprise and shook his head but he did not move away. When Adam continued to stroke his head, he found he liked it and stood still. When Adam moved away Haki followed him a step or two before he decided to return to Hecla.

It was Hecla's way to stick her nose in Adam's pocket if he did not produce the sugar quickly enough to please her. Adam kept the sugar for Hecla in one pocket and the lumps for Haki in the other. Haki watched Hecla trying to push her nose into Adam's pocket. He tried to push his nose in alongside Hecla's. Hecla gave him an indignant push out of her way. Haki looked cross for a moment then gathered up his sticks of legs and frisked round to the other side of Adam. Adam held his pocket invitingly open. Haki hesitated only the barest fraction of a second, then sank his nose into the pocket and pulled out the sugar.

'Good, Haki! Clever beastie!' Adam praised him. Haki tossed his mane as though he were pleased with himself too. This time he let Adam pat his shoulder and fondle him between the ears. Never, after this, did he shrink away from Adam. Soon, when Adam climbed the Hill of Berry, he called for both ponies, 'Hecla! Haki!' and they both came to him. Then, one day, he called only for Haki. Hecla and her foal were lying in a warm patch of grass, asleep in the sun.

'Haki! Haki! Come here!' Adam called.

Haki's ears pricked up. He hesitated, rose, then took two or three steps in Adam's direction before Hecla woke up to the fact that Adam was there with the sugar. She rose to her feet and jostled Haki out of the way, but it was Haki who was first aware of Adam's coming.

Adam held out Haki's sugar. 'You know your name now, laddie! Haki! Haki!' he said affectionately as he caressed the little animal, rubbing his throat and under his mouth. When Adam moved away, Haki followed and thrust his head trustingly under Adam's armpit.

Adam was thrilled with joy at this show of affection.

'Haki! Haki!, you're mine! We belong to each other and you know it!' he whispered to the colt.

This time, when Adam went away down the hill, both Hecla and Haki followed him for a short distance, till Hecla found an interesting patch of grass for grazing. Even then Haki stood looking after Adam for a moment or two before he plunged his head under his mother.

School and work on the croft went on side by side for Adam. Those were the long days of early summer in Shetland when the sun scarcely seemed to set below the horizon before it was dawn again. The simmer dim was the name the Shetland folk gave to the summer twilight, for even at midnight it was possible to see up the hill and for Magnus Cromarty to read his newspaper by the cottage door. Even the hens seemed reluctant to roost and the cock began to crow at an unearthly hour.

'It'll be fine the morn and we can start cutting the peats. It's Saturday and Adam can lend me a hand,' Magnus Cromarty said on a Friday evening in June.

Adam pulled a face but he said nothing. He loved to go down to the shore at Scalloway on a Saturday. The trawlers would have come in with the full tide and be moored at the fish quay. The fishermen stood smoking their pipes and yarning to each other. Down at the King Olaf slipway Ronald Sinclair was painting his boat *The Dawn Wind* and Adam's friend Ian would be helping him. Usually Ronald gave them a brush apiece and they got the job of painting the outside of the wheel-house. Even if there was no painting to be done, the motorboat *Tirrick* usually took the tourists from the hotel a trip round the Island of Trondra. On Saturday there was a chance of a cruise among the sea-voes or firths to see the nesting birds on the cliffs or the seals basking on the rocks. Maybe Mr Smith might take Adam with him as deck hand as he sometimes did. There was always the odd ten pence or so to be earned, helping the tourists with their luggage when they arrived on the bus from Lerwick. Oh, there was plenty for a boy to do in Scalloway on a Saturday! If Magnus Cromarty had decided to cut the peats, though, then it was no use objecting. Peat cutting and stacking had to be done in fine weather and too often there were days of swirling mist in Shetland.

The peat banks lie among the moors. The peat itself is like thick black earth, made by layer upon layer of decayed vegetation. It takes hundreds of years for a peat moss to be formed. It is really the beginning of coal. Like coal, peat will burn, though not so fast and not with a bright flame. It smoulders away for a long time. The islanders use it in place of coal. True, nowadays coal boats bring supplies of coal to Lerwick, and the folk there use electricity too. The crofters in the hills, however, find that coal is dear to buy and that it costs a lot to have it carted from the ports.

'Anyway, what's the use of paying good money for coal when we have our own peats almost at our door for the taking?' the thrifty Mrs Cromarty said, and Magnus agreed with her.

Money was never too plentiful in the Cromarty family. None the less, they did not go hungry. On some days Magnus Cromarty went out with the fishing boats and he always brought herring or haddock back with him. Their small croft provided them with potatoes. Mrs Cromarty kept hens so there was now and again a fowl for boiling and eggs enough. Their field of barley gave them barley meal both for porridge and bursten broonies, the barley meal scones that she baked.

'Make a lot of bursten broonies, Mother. We'll be fair hungry when we come back from the peat-cutting,' Adam begged.

'Aye, they'll be keeping warm in the oven for you,' she promised, 'and there'll be a fish-pie, forbye.'

'Adam's hungry already,' Magnus laughed. 'Come away, laddie! Time we were getting up to the peat banks!'

Mrs Cromarty's hands had already taken up her knitting needles. The needles were stuck in a padded leather belt round her waist and her knitting she carried in a bag-like apron. The minute she had finished any household job she rinsed her hands and dried them and straightaway her needles flew in and out with amazing speed. She was making a Shetland cardigan in fine wool with an intricate yoke pattern in several colours. She carried the pattern in her head, although it was so complicated. It was a pattern she had learned as a girl at her mother's knee, handed down from mother to daughter for many generations. Most Shetland women are skilled knitters, their hands never idle, even knitting as they go from one place to another, or while talking to friends. Mrs Cromarty sold her knitting to a shop in Lerwick, which sold it in turn to the tourists. Many Shetland women helped to keep their families by their knitting. In years to come, whenever Adam thought of his mother when he was far from the Shetlands, he saw her always with the flashing needles in her hands.

Adam and Magnus set off for the peat banks on the Hill of Berry. It was still early morning and the world was wakening in the little town below them. Adam cast a regretful glance at the flagged wharf where the Trondra ferry was already waiting. The Island of Trondra lay green and fresh in the blue waters of the East Voe. White yachts lay at anchor in the tideway. Half-a-dozen small islets starred the bay. The sea creamed round the rocky shores of the Skerries and Green Holm and Merry Holm. Many was the time that Adam had pulled out in a boat to the islands taking holiday-makers to see the haunts of the sea birds, gannets and herring-gulls, kittiwakes and shag.

'Come on, Adam! Forget the money you might have been earning from the tourists. There'll be plenty more days for that during the school holidays.' Magnus laughed at his son. 'The peat-cutting's the thing today if you don't want to freeze this winter.'

They reached the peat bank. The soil had been cut away to a depth of two feet, revealing the black peat.

'Shall I be getting a turn with the tushkar?' Adam asked his father.

The tushkar was a spade specially made for cutting peat. It had a wide sharp blade with a rim at the haft which prevented the peat from sliding off when it was lifted.

'Aye, lad, you shall have a turn if you work hard at the stacking,' Magnus promised.

He made two sharp cuts about ten inches apart, then cut a slice of peat about four inches thick neatly from between the two cuts. Magnus lifted and flung it to the top of the peat bank. Adam set it on edge. The next peat he set at right angles to the first one, making a kind of herring-bone pattern all along the edge of the peat bank. The wind would blow through the stacked peats and dry them.

Adam and his father worked in silence. It was a tough job cutting peats and did not leave much breath for talking. Not till the sun was high in the sky did they stop for the bread and cheese and flask of tea that Mrs Cromarty had put up for them. They sat down under the shelter of a heather bank, out of the wind that so often blows in Shetland.

Just as Adam was finishing the last crumbs of cheese he felt a gentle nuzzling at his neck. He looked around quickly and stood up. 'Look who's here!' he cried. It was Hecla with her foal.

She tried to push her nose into Adam's right-hand pocket while Haki nudged with his nose at Adam's left side.

'What are they after?' Magnus Cromarty asked, but there was an amused gleam in his eye that showed he had guessed.

Adam shamefacedly drew a lump of sugar from each pocket and offered them in each hand to Hecla and Haki.

His father laughed. 'So that's where your mother's sugar has been going? She said we seemed to be getting through an awful lot. She thought *you* were the sweet-tooth.'

'I – I'll buy her a pound at the store if I earn any money from the tourists next week,' Adam promised.

'Och, laddie, your mother 'll no' grudge you a lump or two of sugar now and again for the ponies.'

'Well, it's not just "now and again". I take sugar to them every day,' Adam admitted honestly. 'They each get two lumps. Watch this!' He held up two fingers and cried, 'Haki! Two!' At once the colt came to Adam and reached his head up towards his hand. Adam gave him the second lump and rubbed

25

his nose affectionately. The colt did not back away but licked his hand.

'He seems well acquainted with you,' Magnus Cromarty remarked drily.

Adam was suddenly encouraged to do a thing he had never attempted before. He slipped his left arm under the neck of the colt and his right arm over his back, holding Haki's flank with his right hand. Haki was startled and tried to back away but Adam cuddled him more firmly. The colt felt he was imprisoned and flung his head up in the air and tried to buck, to get rid of Adam's arm. His neck muscles grew taut. Adam held on, talking quietly.

'Quiet, now, Haki! You're all right, laddie! Nothing is going to hurt you. Keep still now!'

Hecla watched warily, looking anxiously at the foal. Haki still tried to break away but Adam would not let him go. It was a contest of wills. He had to come out of it the winner if Haki was to learn obedience and have confidence in him. Then Adam had an inspiration. He hummed the tune he always whistled when he approached Hecla and Haki as he came up the hill. The foal pricked up his ears and ceased to struggle. This sound was something Haki knew, a pleasant sound that usually meant there would soon be the sweet taste of sugar on his tongue. He struggled again but not so violently as he had done at first. He ceased to buck and curve his back, though he still stretched his neck upwards tensely.

'Steady now, Haki!' Adam said quietly. With his

26

left hand he stroked the tightened muscles of the little animal's throat, singing softly to him the tune he knew so well.

The little colt began to relax but Adam did not let go his hold. Haki began to like the soothing feel of Adam's hand at his throat. He no longer trembled. His throat muscles slackened. At last he stood still and passive in Adam's encircling arms. He gave a gentle whinny and nosed at Adam's hands. He had found out that, though Adam held him so he could not break away, no harm had come to him, but rather comfort and love.

'You've mastered him. Adam,' Magnus Cromarty said with approval. 'He's learned a lesson he'll not forget. He's yours now.'

Adam let go his hold on the colt and plunged his hand into his pocket and brought out the rewarding lump of sugar and held it out to Haki. 'Three!' he said. 'Three, Haki!'

'Mercy me, lad! You'll have the animal counting next!'

'I mean to!' Adam replied quite seriously. 'Already he knows he gets two lumps of sugar when I visit them on the hill. Soon he'll learn he gets a third lump when he's quiet and obedient when I handle him.'

'It's not a pound of sugar but a sackful you'll need to buy for your mother,' Magnus chuckled. 'You'd better get a job for the holidays on Mr Smith's boat.'

For another couple of hours they continued cutting the peats. Hecla and Haki still hung around and watched them. Mr Cromarty stopped wielding his tushkar for a minute.

'You know, Adam, it might be a good idea to let Haki see his mother being led down the hill to the croft. It would get him used to seeing her in a halter with a leading rein. Then when the time comes for him to wear a halter, it will not seem a strange thing. Animals have more intelligence than folk think. Away with you down to the croft and fetch a halter up.'

Adam went fleeing down the hill as fast as his legs would carry him while his father carried on cutting the peats. Adam soon returned carrying the halter and leading rein. Hecla and Haki were still grazing beside the peat bank. Adam whistled his tune and both the mare and the foal lifted their heads at once. They came to him at his call. Hecla seemed rather surprised when Adam strapped the halter on to her head and attached the leading rein to the swivel ring but she made no resistance. Haki watched with great eyes and gave an uncertain whinny and dived under his mother.

'The colt's a bit nervous of what you're doing,' Magnus said, 'but it's time Hecla got used to working again too. Her holiday has lasted long enough. Lead her down the hill, Adam.'

'Come away, Hecla!' Adam gave a tug at the rein and Hecla shook off Haki impatiently and followed Adam. Haki stood still for a minute, then rushed to fall in at Hecla's heels.

Magnus Cromarty shouldered his tushkar. 'You can come back after your supper and stack what's left of the peats,' he told Adam. 'Take Hecla right down to the stable and into it.'

'Will you be keeping her there the night?' Adam asked in surprise. The mare was rarely kept in the stable. She usually roamed the hill.

'No. You can drive her up the hill again after supper. We shall have to fasten Haki in the stable for a while when it comes to the weaning of him.'

'But that will not be for three months at least yet,' Adam pointed out.

'True! It is a good thing, though, to let him be seeing the stable and getting used to being in it now and again. Then, when the time comes for him to leave his mother, he will not be so scared of the place and try to kick his way out of it.'

The colt followed the little procession down the Hill of Berry. More than once he stopped and whinnied as though to say that he wished to be fed. Adam led Hecla on firmly and Haki caught up with her in a rush of his long thin legs.

At last they reached the stable. Hecla hesitated a moment as if she, too, felt that she was losing her freedom. A sharp tug at her halter brought her into the stable. The foal nickered with fear at the thought of entering the narrow place, so different from the wide hill-side. He was even more fearful of losing the comfort of his mother, however, so he plunged after her out of the sunlight. Adam tied up Hecla so she was quite comfortable and rubbed her

29

nose and patted her shoulder. Haki dashed at once to feed from his mother, not so much because he was hungry as for the comfort of the warm feel of her milk in his mouth.

'Give Hecla a small feed of oats and leave them in the stable while you have your supper,' Magnus told Adam. 'Away in, lad! I can smell your mother's good baking out here.'

Mrs Cromarty lifted the bursten broonies from the flat 'girdle', like a frying pan without a rim, which swung by a chain over the fire. Then she took the fish pie, rich with cheese, from the fireside oven, while Adam and his father washed away the peat grime from hands and faces at the kitchen sink. They sat down at the deal table with the white linen cloth to eat their simple supper that was fit for a king.

3

Haki leaves his mother

The summer slipped by quickly for both Adam and Haki. Adam watched Haki thrive and grow from a tiny pony not much bigger than a dog till he was more than half the size of Hecla. Every day Adam visited them on the hill-side where they roamed freely. Haki soon came bounding down the hill to meet him, often in advance of Hecla.

Adam handled the colt every day. After a while he ceased to struggle at all and seemed to welcome the feel of Adam's arms about him and liked to hear Adam's soothing gentle voice.

Adam tried a new exercise with Haki. With his hand resting on Haki's cheek and the other hand on his neck he gently turned the colt's head from right to left. Next he shifted his hands and moved the head from left to right. At first Haki's muscles stiffened with nervousness and he snorted and shook his head. Adam tried again. He repeated the movements several times, talking quietly all the time.

'Haki, you silly colt! Don't you know I'm trying to help you? Some day you'll have to submit to a halter and bridle. This will make it easier for you when the time comes. You will have learned to turn your head where I want you to go and we shall understand each other better. Quiet, now, Haki!' He stroked the little pony's muzzle.

Before long Haki permitted Adam to handle him without any signs of fear. When Haki stayed quiet and happy under his hands Adam was ready to try another kind of handling.

'When you are frightened, Haki, you strike out with your legs and hoofs. You must learn to let me touch these too without striking at me,' Adam told him.

Adam started rubbing at Haki's shoulder, moving

his hand in a widening circle. Haki liked this petting. He stood still. Adam massaged Haki lightly from the shoulder to the knee. Still Haki did not move. Pressing gently, Adam moved his hand downwards from the knee to the fetlock, cupping the bone there in his hand. This time Haki picked up his foot rather sharply but Adam had been expecting this and he held on. Haki looked rather helplessly at him, not knowing what to do. He could not kick when Adam held on so firmly and he needed the other foot to stand on. He fidgeted a little and tried to move backwards but Adam retained his grip. He talked kindly to the pony. All at once Haki knew he did not want to kick Adam; that he liked Adam to talk to him and handle him. Confidence grew between them.

One day Adam put his arm over Haki's back and tapped him gently on the flank.

'Come with me, Haki!' he said and pulled on the animal's neck. At first Haki stood stock-still, not knowing what was required of him. The slight pull on his neck urged him forwards.

'Come!' Adam's voice was insistent. Haki took a step or two forward with Adam's arm about his neck.

'That's the way of it, Haki! That's the way!' Adam was delighted. 'When you are ready for a halter you will have little fear of it. Now you must learn to stop, too, when I tell you.'

Adam was carrying a short stick. It was one his father used to urge along the sheep and ponies, but

Adam would never dream of striking Haki with it. Instead he held it in front of the little animal and said 'Stop!' At the same time he held Haki back by the arm around his neck.

Haki backed, reared a little and clattered his hoofs.

'Quiet now, lad! You did as I told you. Good, Haki! Good! We'll try it again soon, and next time you'll not be so startled.'

Down the hill they went together, Adam's arm still about Haki. The little colt did not attempt to break loose. This time Adam swung the stick so that Haki could see it and get used to it. Once again he brought it up like a bar before Haki and called, 'Stop!' This time, though Haki clattered his hoofs, he did not try to rear. He stopped with chest against the stick and snorted and shook his head, impatient at the restraint.

Again and again they moved forward and Adam halted the animal by the stick as a bar. Always he gave the word, 'Stop, Haki!' at the same time. Soon Haki had grown to know both the stick and the word of command.

For several days Adam practised this exercise with Haki. The colt learned to stop obediently and not to fidget too much. Then, one day Adam did *not* hold the stick in front of him but called 'Stop, Haki!' and Haki did as he was told.

'Yes, boy, you'll take kindly to the halter,' Adam said. But it was not the time for the halter yet. Haki had first to be weaned. He still plunged to Hecla for comfort and warm milk, though every day he grew more independent. He cropped the sparse grass and the heather shoots alongside Hecla. He followed her down to the shore. Together they munched at the moss-like sea-weed which grew on the rocks and which every Shetland pony likes to eat. They browsed along the fringe of sea-weed washed up by the tide. Haki gambolled over the sand in wider and wider circles round his mother, no longer afraid to leave her side. Hecla still kept a wary eye on him and went after him when she thought he was becoming too venturesome. She was growing a little impatient of him, though, and of his continual demands for her milk. When she thought he had had enough she shook him aside and moved on to another patch of grass.

'The time is coming for the colt to be weaned,' Magnus Cromarty decided. 'We will wait till the peats have been brought in.'

All summer the work had gone on of stacking and turning the peats for the wind to dry them. By early September it was time to carry the peats to the croft and store them in the lean-to beside the house.

'Bring Hecla down from the hill,' Magnus told Adam. 'Take up the halter for her.'

When Hecla saw Adam approaching with the halter in his hand she knew that her spell of liberty was over. She kicked up her heels and disappeared over the heather knoll.

Adam laughed. 'All right, my lassie! I know a

34

trick to make you obey.' He paused at the top of the heather knoll and called, not for Hecla, but Haki.

Haki had gone bounding after Hecla but at the sound of Adam's voice, he faltered and turned.

'Come back, Hecla!' Adam shouted, but Hecla paid no heed.

'Come, Haki!' Adam called next.

Haki looked from one to the other, torn between the instinct to follow his mother and the habit of obedience to Adam. In the end it was Adam who won, Haki turned away from Hecla and trotted down the hill-side towards the boy.

'Good lad! Good Haki!' Adam rewarded him with a lump of sugar.

Hecla watched her colt. She saw Adam hold the sugar to Haki's mouth and she was filled with jealousy. Back she came, plunging down the hill. She made straight for Adam's pocket and pushed her son out of the way. Quick as lightning Adam had the halter over her head and the halter shank snapped in place. Adam held the halter lead in his right hand and pushed at her withers.

Hecla knew she was beaten. She fell into step beside Adam and Haki followed behind. Adam led them to the farm.

'Was Hecla a bit fresh?' Magnus Cromarty asked.

'Aye. She's no' liking the thought of work again,' Adam grinned.

'These beasts are nigh human,' Magnus agreed.

'Weel, put the kishies on her and we'll be off to the peat banks to lift the peats.'

The kishies were two deep pannier baskets that were strapped across Hecla's back, one hanging on each side. Once Hecla had submitted to the halter, she made no fuss about the kishies. She nodded her head up and down a few times as if to say, 'What's the use of bothering?'

All that day Adam led Hecla up to the peat banks, loaded the kishies and guided Hecla back to the croft. Haki followed his mother, stopping when Adam and Hecla stopped, watching curiously while the peats were loaded into the baskets.

When the day's work was over Hecla and Haki were turned loose to graze on the hill-side again.

For several days the loading of the peats went on. Other crofters came with their ponies to their neighbouring peat banks too. There was a regular procession up and down the hill. At last the evening came when the last of the peats were brought in.

'The foal is big enough to look after himself now,' Magnus Cromarty said. 'You take Haki and shut him up in the stable. I'll drive Hecla back up the hill. Later on, when Haki has settled down a bit, you can give him a mash of oats and bran and a drink of cow's milk.'

Adam put his arm about Haki and gave the command the pony knew so well, 'Come, Haki!' Obediently Haki followed him into the stable. Adam gave him his lump of sugar then bolted the bottom half-door of the stable, leaving the top half open. Haki

had been used to coming into the stable with Hecla while the kishies were emptied, so the stable was no new place to him. When he found the half-door of the stable shut, he tried to poke his head over the top, but he was still too small to do that. He pranced on his hind legs and caught a glimpse of Adam disappearing into the house. Now the colt knew indeed that he was alone. He whinnied with indignation. He had never been locked in a stable before.

Adam heard Haki's whinny and he hesitated with his foot on the door-step. He turned and went back. For a while he leaned over the half-door, talking to the colt. Haki tossed his head questioningly and clattered his hoofs.

'It's all right, Haki! You'll not be here alone for long. It's just till you get used to growing up and being away from Hecla. I'll be bringing you your supper soon.'

Haki quietened down while Adam talked to him and nosed along to sniff at Adam's hand. When Adam left him the colt soon became restive again. Hecla was shut into the hill field behind the farm, hemmed in by wire fence and gate. She neighed after her colt. Haki heard her and whinnied in return, clattering with his hoofs at the half-door.

The neighing and whinnying went on like call and echo. Adam ate his supper in silence, listening and looking unhappy.

'The colt's not settling down very well,' Magnus Cromarty remarked. 'Take him his mash as soon as

38

you've eaten your meal, Adam. Maybe he'll quieten down when his stomach is full. He'll be missing Hecla's milk.'

Adam hastened over his last mouthful and left the table. In the back-kitchen he stirred a mash of oats and bran into a soft paste. Then he warmed milk in a pan and poured it into a clean scrubbed pail.

He set down the two pails near the stable door. Haki heard his footsteps and was waiting, poised for flight. As soon as the half-door was opened, he bolted out. Adam was standing in his way. Though he was almost knocked over by the colt's rush, his arms went out and grabbed Haki round the neck. Haki reared and pranced, but Adam held on.

'Quiet! Quiet now, Haki!' he implored him.

The little animal was driven frantic by his need for Hecla and he lashed out with his small hoofs. One of them caught Adam on the knee but luckily he was only slightly cut. Adam held on. Haki whinnied again, a whinny like a whimpering child.

'Oh, Haki! Haki!' Adam almost sobbed, but he would not let go of the struggling colt. At last, rubbing and stroking Haki's shoulders he went through the movements the colt knew so well. Haki became quieter. Adam scarcely dared to hope the pony would obey him but he turned Haki's head towards the stable and urged him on.

'Go in, Haki! Go in!'

The habit of obedience was strong in Haki. Of his own accord he turned and walked back into the

39

stable. Adam snatched up the two pails and followed him. He was only barely aware of his victory.

Adam put the bucket of warm milk before Haki. He thrust the colt's nose into it. Haki lifted his head, looked surprised, but licked his lips. Another second and he had his nose down in the bucket. When Adam thought he had had enough, he took away the bucket and put the pail of bran mash in its place. Haki sniffed at the bran mash. It was new to him but it smelt good. He licked at it with his rough tongue. Strange food, but Adam had set it before him and he trusted Adam! Soon he began to eat.

Adam reached down an armful of straw for bedding. When he fastened the stable door behind him, the colt was already comfortably settled among it.

In the middle of the night Adam awoke with a jerk. There was a plaintive whinnying coming from the stable, a lost child crying for the warmth of his mother. Adam listened a while, then could bear it no longer. He jumped from his bed and threw on his clothes. Adam paused at the top of the narrow steep staircase. From his parents' room came only the sound of their deep breathing. He tiptoed down the stairs and held his breath as he turned the key in the squeaky lock. Another instant and he had crossed the threshold. He pulled the door shut behind him and crossed through the shaft of moonlight that lay across the open yard of the croft. This time he took care to open the stable door only sufficiently to let him squeeze in, so that Haki could not go charging past him. Once in, he opened the top half-door so he could see the colt by the moon's light.

Haki stood there, unhappy, trembling a little. He was like a child who had wakened alone in a strange place. Adam's arms went round him.

'You poor wee creature! You can't think what's happened to you and you want your mother,' Adam whispered to him. 'Stop shaking now. *I'm* staying with you. You'll always have *me*.' There was a fierce determination in Adam's voice.

Haki grew still again and Adam knelt among the straw, drawing the little animal down beside him.

When Magnus Cromarty found them early next morning they were both asleep. Adam lay with his arms about the colt's neck and Haki's muzzle was against Adam's cheek. Magnus smiled a little: then he shook his head.

'Aye, laddie, you set great store by your pony,' he said under his breath. 'But it doesna do. It doesna do to get over fond of a beast. It comes the harder when you have to part.' He wakened Adam with great gentleness.

In the months that followed Haki ran in the fields with the other young ponies belonging to other crofts. Hecla joined the mares on the rough hill-side pasture. Even when the winter gales swept Shetland the ponies stayed out in the open. They pawed at the ground and freed the heather and grass from a light covering of snow. Only when the frost overlaid the snow like a sheet of iron did Magnus Cromarty bring the animals down to the croft to give them hay.

Little by little the image of his mother faded from Haki's mind. He loved racing around and the rough-and-tumble with other colts. He learned to stand his ground, too, and to rear on his hind legs and lash out with his forefeet if other ponies seemed aggressive.

Hecla, too, began to forget Haki. In the spring she would have another colt to mother. A quiet life browsing with the other mares suited her well as the winter wore on.

There was never a day went by but Adam visited Haki on the hill-side. Even in the winter dark when Haki heard his voice he left the other ponies and came bounding to Adam. Adam always stroked and fondled him, turning his head this way and that and lifting one foot after another. Adam invented new games for them. He would lift the right forefoot and call out 'One!' Then he numbered off each foot in turn like a drill sergeant. The time came when Haki found fun in the game for himself. He recognized each of his feet by the number. When Adam cried 'Three!' up would come his right leg from the ground.

Adam taught him 'Right!' and 'Left!' too and when he rapped out these commands Haki would turn of his own accord.

There was another exercise that Haki loved. Adam had learned as a small boy to play the bag-pipes. Magnus Cromarty was a powerful piper himself and had taught Adam to play as soon as he was old enough to handle a chanter. Adam had a natural gift for music and he often took the pipes up the hill-side to practise. Haki learned to associ-ate the sound of the bagpipes with Adam. He came cantering to Adam whenever he heard them. Often, as Adam marched up and down playing, Haki followed at his heels, turning when Adam turned. This gave Adam another idea.

'It seems you like music too, Haki. Could I not be teaching you to march?'

Adam began by whistling *Scotland the Brave* and taking Haki's forefeet in his hands and drum-ming them up and down to the beat of the tune. Soon Haki began to paw and drum whenever he heard the same tune. Before long, when Adam picked up the pipes and played and marched, Haki moved his little hoofs to the beat of the music and marched too.

'Adam's playing that tune a mighty lot,' Mrs Cromarty remarked one day when the skirl of Adam's music came to her from the hill-side.

'He has a reason,' Magnus Cromarty grinned. 'Come you to the door, woman, and you will see for yourself.'

Mrs Cromarty stood at the door and shielded her eyes from the glare of the setting sun. Along the ridge of the hill marched Adam, playing his pipes, and after him, his feet keeping time with Adam's and with the rhythm of the music, pranced Haki!

'I would never have believed it possible. The lad's bewitched the wee beast,' she exclaimed. 'It's an uncanny-like thing, that!'

'Uncanny it may be but the lad has a wonderful power over the colt. He's trained him to do other things too and never a halter nor rope near the animal,' Magnus declared.

'I'm not so sure that I like Adam to be so wrapped up in that pony. He is not as much with other lads in Scalloway on Saturdays now. Ian Sinclair comes up here, it's true, but Adam does not go and work on *The Dawn Wind* as he used to do,' Mrs Cromarty remarked.

'Fegs! There's not much doing down at the shipyard in the winter months. Wait till the geese start flying north and Ian's brother begins the painting again on the ship. You'll find Adam will be down with them and forgetting the colt.'

'Maybe you're right, but I have a queer feeling here about it.' She touched her heart. 'There is something tells me that Adam will never be parted from Haki, come what may!'

In the spring Magnus Cromarty was busy with the lambing. He brought the ewes down from the cold hill-side so that they could give birth to their lambs in the comfort of the shed near to the croft. For days the farm echoed to the plaintive bleating of lambs.

Sometimes, when the wind from the Arctic blew like a knife over Shetland, the new-born lambs had to be brought into the warm kitchen if they were to survive. Many a day Adam returned from school to find his mother feeding a lamb from a baby's feeding bottle. Up on the hill-side, though, the Shetland ponies scraped away snow to find the new springing heather shoots. Hecla was coming near the time when she would have another foal.

One day, when Adam was sitting at his home-work, he heard his parents talking in the back-kitchen.

'There will soon be too many ponies for them all to find food on the hill-side,' Magnus Cromarty re-marked. 'Some of them will have to go to Lerwick to the pony sales. There will likely be buyers from Scotland and England too.'

'Will you be taking the boy's pony?' Mrs Crom-arty sounded anxious.

'Not yet. We can wait another year or so till he is bigger. He is a good colt, though. He would bring in a lot of money.'

'But you *gave* him to Adam,' Mrs Cromarty re-minded her husband.

'Aye, aye, so I did, but maybe the boy could be using the money to help him on in the world. It will not be long now before he leaves the school. Then he must find a job. It might be that he will go into the office of a shipping company in Lerwick, now, or into a bank. That means he will need a good decent suit of dark cloth and where is the money to come from to provide that? It's little enough I make off the farm nowadays.'

'Would you not want Adam to help you on the croft?' his wife asked.

'Och, woman, what future is there in that? Adam may want to marry when he grows older. There is little enough from the farm to keep one family, let alone two. No, it is out into the world Adam must go.'

'I cannot see Adam sitting in an office or a bank. He has always been a lad for the animals and the outdoor work. Maybe, though, you could get a job for him on the trawlers, fishing?'

'Maybe. I will be speaking with Ronald Sinclair, though he was saying they will not be able to take on more than one or two lads.'

Adam flew out of the door and up the hill-side. He had hardly breath left to whistle and call Haki. When the pony came to him his arms went round it in a fierce protective hug.

'They shall never take you away from me, Haki! Never! And I will *not* go to Lerwick or in a fishing boat where I shall be parted from you and you will forget me! I will not!'

4

A contest of wills

The summer Adam Cromarty was due to leave school Haki had grown almost to the full size of a Shetland pony. From the ground to the top of his withers he was just thirty-four inches high. Magnus Cromarty looked at him with approval.

'Aye, he's a right neat size. The smaller, the better! He'll not grow more than a couple of inches now. That'll bring him to just the right size for a show pony. He's got a good heavy mane and tail too. He carries his head well up. I wouldna be surprised, Adam, but you'd take a prize with him at the show in Lerwick.'

Adam's eyes sparkled. 'Do you really think he's good enough?'

'Aye, lad, I do. But you'll have to break him in to saddle and bridle first. Can you make him open his mouth for me?'

'Oh, aye! Watch this!' Adam tickled the corners of Haki's mouth. Haki drew back his lips as if smiling and opened his mouth. 'See! He'll even let me put my hand inside his mouth.'

'Well!' Magnus was quite impressed. He peered inside Haki's mouth. 'He's lost his milk teeth but the incisors are well grown now. Aye, he's got a good mouth. Be careful you're not rough with him

47

when you break him in to the halter and bridle.'

'I'd never be rough with Haki. He trusts me. I'll break him in on the soft field near the stream so that if he falls he'll not hurt himself.'

'Good idea!'

Adam started by putting a head collar on the colt each morning and taking it off at night. At first Haki tried to back away from the collar but Adam laid hold of his mane and placed the collar firmly in position. Haki shook his head hard.

'It's no use struggling, Haki! You will have to wear the collar. You may as well submit now,' Adam told him firmly.

When Haki found he could not shake off the collar he stopped trying. When he saw Adam coming with the collar, though, he kicked out with his back legs and tried to move away. It was a tussle of wills between them, but Adam always won. Once the collar was on, Adam always gave Haki his lump of sugar and Haki licked Adam's hands, as if to show there was no ill-feeling between them. After a while the backing and the head-shaking became only a gesture of protest. Then one day, to Adam's astonishment, when he approached with the collar, Haki came forward. He bent his head and let Adam put the collar on with no fuss at all. Haki had found out that the sooner he submitted, the sooner Adam gave him that tasty lump of sugar.

It was not quite such an easy victory when it came to breaking in the pony to being led by a rein. Adam turned Haki into the field near the stream where the ground was soft. He took a long webbing lunge rein that his father used when breaking ponies. He attached it to the halter. Haki did not make any move but his eyes flicked sideways as if he asked himself, 'What is Adam up to now?'

Adam tried to lead Haki forwards. Haki showed the whites of his eyes and dug his hoofs into the soft ground.

'Come on, Haki!' Adam said persuasively but Haki was having none of it. He shook his head obstinately. He found he could not get rid of the rein. Adam gave a little tug. Haki refused to budge. Adam knew it was no use tugging away at the rein. The pony would only become more obstinate. He slackened the rein and waited.

Haki could not understand why Adam was just standing there: why nothing happened. Curiosity got the better of him. He took a few paces forward towards Adam. At once Adam tightened his hold on the rein and walked ahead. Haki followed. Till he was half-way round the field all went happily. Adam began to think he was going to have an easy victory. Then Haki felt the slight pull on the rein. He sensed he was losing his freedom and he became annoyed. It was as though he said to himself, 'I'll show Adam!' He bucked, lifting all four feet off the ground. Then he set off galloping round the field as hard as he could go. He was trying to shake Adam off. Adam held on to the rein like grim death. Haki tugged him here and there but still Adam held on, acting like a brake on Haki's mad movements. Adam was out of breath but he jerked out, 'It's no use, Haki! I'll never let go!'

Haki made one more frantic effort. Then Adam stumbled! As he fell, he still clutched the rein. Haki continued his mad career. This time, however, the pull on the rein was tighter. He looked back. There was Adam on the ground being hauled over the tussocky grass but still holding on to that rein. Haki faltered in his stride. There was something wrong with Adam. Adam should be standing on his feet and not lying on the ground. He stopped abruptly. Adam, the breath beaten out of him, still lay on his side. Haki turned and came back. He bent over Adam and licked his face. Adam came to his senses with Haki nuzzling him. He was still clutching the rein. Slowly he rose to his feet. Haki stood still, watching Adam as he gathered the rein into a bunch in his hand.

'Now, Haki, come along!' Adam said firmly, giving a shake to the rein. Obediently Haki trotted after him!

They went round and round the field. With each circuit Adam felt more triumphant. Haki was quite docile. There had not been much difficulty in the breaking-in after all. As Haki trotted along he became more and more *bored*. All at once he decided that he had had quite enough of it. He stopped in his tracks. The rope between him and Adam tightened with a jerk. Haki slid along the ground, sat down, then rolled over. Adam came rushing back to look at him. Haki lifted his head, turned it to one side and looked at Adam. Adam could have sworn there was a kind of smirk on Haki's face. It was though he said, 'Well what are you going to do about that now?'

'Get up, Haki!' Adam said, giving a jerk to the rein.

Haki remained on the ground. Adam tried again but still the pony refused to rise. It was to be another clash of wills.

'Right!' Adam said. 'If you want it that way, Haki, we'll play it that way.'

Adam deliberately sat down on the grass a short distance away. Haki raised his head to look at him. The rein lay slack between them but the other end of it was still in Adam's hand. Both of them stayed on the ground, each waiting for the other to move.

It was Haki who first found the situation boring. After a few minutes he lifted his head and whinnied softly in a coaxing way. Adam did not reply but he smiled to himself. Haki tried again, this time louder. Still no move from Adam! Then the colt rolled over on to his legs and stood up. Adam gave no sign that he had noticed. Then Haki approached across the field at a walking pace. As he came nearer he pretended to crop the grass. Adam watched him out of the corner of his eye. The only move he made was to haul in the slack of the rein but not so much that the pony could feel the pull on it. Haki came nearer and nearer. Adam sat up but still he did not rise to his feet. At last Haki reached him, put a head on his shoulder and made a snuffling sound.

'Want to be friends now, do you?' Adam asked, rubbing the colt between his ears. In a couple of minutes he rose to his feet.

'Right! We'll try again,' he said.

It seemed as if Haki understood. He walked obediently behind Adam. Now and again Adam quickened his pace and Haki stirred his stumps too. He preferred it when Adam moved fast. Adam broke into a run and the colt trotted just after him. Adam shortened the rein a little so that Haki could feel more strain on it. After a while Adam settled down into a slow walking pace again. This did not suit Haki at all. He whinnied in protest but Adam paid no heed. Haki decided it was time to lie down on the job again! Down he went on to his knees, tucked in his back legs and rolled over!

Adam was annoyed and gave a sharp jerk to the rein but Haki would not rise. Down went Adam on to the grass too and once more they played the waiting game.

This time Adam was sitting beside the fence where he had left his bagpipes. He had a sudden inspiration. He looped the rein round his upper arm, stretched out his hands and picked up the bagpipes. When Haki heard the drones throbbing in the bag and the opening skirl of the pipes he pricked up his ears. He knew what was coming. Adam rose to his feet. The first chords of *Scotland the Brave* resounded over the meadow. By the time Adam had played the first bars, 'Hark! Hark! The pipes are calling!' Haki was on his feet too. The pipes were indeed calling him!

Adam started out on the slow strutting march, keeping the rein looped round his upper arm. It stretched taut. Haki did not resist. He fell into step behind Adam with a curious rolling stamping movement of his legs. Solemnly they marched up and down the field.

Whenever Haki developed his lying-down tactics during the next hour, Adam sat down too and gave him five minutes' breathing space. Then once more the bagpipes struck up their tune. It acted like magic on Haki. He never failed to rise to his feet and move round the field at Adam's bidding.

Up at the croft Magnus Cromarty heard the sound of the pipes frequently starting and stopping.

'Whatever's the lad at?' he said to his wife. 'He's supposed to be breaking in that colt. I'll away down to the field and take a wee look what's happening.'

He arrived in time to see Adam and Haki both rise from the ground to the strains of *Scotland the Brave* and commence their solemn march round the field.

Adam looked up to see his father leaning on the fence and laughing. He broke off the pipe music and stood still. So did Haki, obedient and composed.

'I've got the measure of him, father!' Adam cried. 'Haki's broken now to the halter and the rein.'

'Aye, I can see that. Well, it's the first time a colt has ever been broken to the music o' the pipes,' he chuckled. 'It's an unusual way of going about it but I must grant it seems to work.'

The next step in Haki's training was putting a saddle on him. Adam began by laying a folded horse-blanket across his back and hanging two kishies over it. Perhaps Haki had a memory of seeing those on Hecla for he did not object. Adam began by carrying light weights in them at first, a few turnips from the store; some hay from the stack. Haki obeyed orders; stood still when he was told; moved on when Adam gave the word. Then Adam exchanged the horse-cloth and kishies for a saddle. When Adam strapped on the saddle Haki merely turned his head sideways and watched curiously. He gave a snort or two which may have expressed disdain. Adam let him wear the saddle for several days, taking it off at night and putting it on in the morning till Haki got quite used to the whole business. It was a different matter, though, when Adam tried to sit astride the saddle!

Shetland ponies are so small that a grown man can mount one and have a foot touching the ground on each side. Adam was a well-grown lad and he threw a leg over Haki's back. Haki's shock of astonishment made Adam laugh out aloud. The pony turned his head and gave him an indignant look.

Adam had the reins in his hand. He gave them a shake and said, 'Come up, Haki!'

This was too much for Haki! He flung up his hind legs and bucked. Adam had been prepared for this. He held on to the reins grimly and gripped Haki's sides with his knees. Though he slipped forward he held on to Haki's neck. Haki shook himself vigorously as though he could get rid of Adam that way. It had no effect. Adam was still on his back. Then Haki lifted up his front hoofs and pawed the air. That took Adam by surprise and he almost slipped off Haki's rump. He managed to grip his mane just in time. For a moment Haki stood still as though thinking up the next move.

'Come up, Haki!' Adam ordered again.

From force of habit Haki obeyed and walked half-way round the field. Adam began to think he was going to have an easy victory. He had counted without Haki's powers of invention. Haki had tried several ways of getting Adam off his back and none of them had worked. He must try something different. He went another round of the field, then, all of a sudden he went down on his knees, lowered his head and flung Adam over it!

To his surprise Adam found himself sprawling on the grass. It was a good thing the ground was soft. He was still holding on to the reins, however. Haki rose to his feet but he could not get away. Adam also rose ruefully. The two stood staring at each other face to face. Haki lowered his head and looked so ashamed that Adam had to laugh.

'You got the better of me that time, Haki,' he said, 'but don't think you've won, my lad!'

He stepped alongside Haki and, before Haki realized what Adam was doing, he had thrown his leg over the saddle again. This time he gripped hard with his knees and shortened the rein. He was ready for all Haki's tricks now.

Haki went through his whole programme; bucking; trying to slide Adam sideways and backwards; shaking hard and then the final item of trying to throw Adam over his head. Adam had been waiting for this trick. As soon as he saw the pony's head going down and felt his hind legs coming up, he pulled sharply on the shortened reins Haki's head was jerked back. His hoofs came down on the ground again. He tried the trick a second time but Adam was ready for him. Again he failed. Adam clung to him like a burr. Once more they resumed a gentle walk round the field. Several times Haki tried to dislodge Adam. Adam slid about on his back but he always managed to hold on. At last Haki gave a final shake, then turned his head to look at Adam. It was as though he said, 'What? Still there?'

Adam laughed out aloud. 'Aye, I'm still on your back, Haki, and here I mean to stay.'

Perhaps it was Adam's laugh; perhaps it was his confident voice, but all at once Haki realized that Adam was master. He gave in and attempted no more cavorting. Adam rode him round and round the field till the colt was quite docile and obeyed every command, turning right or left as Adam ordered. He had had his lesson but Adam wanted to make sure of it. He paused by the gate leading from the field to the moorland. There he dismounted, opened the gate and Haki walked through.

'Stand still, Haki!' Adam commanded in a very strong voice.

Haki obediently stood still.

Adam shut the gate behind him, approached Haki and mounted again. Beyond the merest shake Haki submitted.

'Now we will ride along the hill-side,' Adam told him. 'Come up, Haki!'

Haki breasted the hill carrying Adam. When they reached a level stretch of short turf Adam gave Haki his head. He slapped him gently on the flank. Haki began to move more quickly. Soon he was trotting, then cantering. As he picked up his hoofs neatly he felt the firm grip of Adam's knees in his sides. All at once Haki knew he liked it; that it was good to have Adam on his back, that he belonged to Adam. For Adam, too, the winning of the colt was a joy as well as a triumph. He knew now that the pony loved and trusted him. He knew too that he could never bear to be parted from Haki.

The summer term at school was drawing to a close. This would be the last term for Adam, for on his birthday in July he would be fifteen years old. It was the last term for his friend Ian too.

'Have you got fixed up with a job yet, Adam?' Ian asked.

Adam shook his head. 'No. What about you?'

'Oh, I'll be going fishing in *The Dawn Wind* with Ronald. That's been settled for a long time. My father left me a share in the boat, you know.'

Ian's father had died five years earlier and Ian lived with his elder brother Ronald and his wife.

'Will you be working with your father on the croft?' he asked Adam.

Adam shook his head. 'The croft isn't enough to support us all. My father says I've to look for a job in Lerwick.'

'What at?'

'Oh, an office or shop, maybe. There's nothing here for me in Scalloway.'

'I've heard tell there are not many jobs for young folk in Lerwick either,' Ian said with a shake of his head.

'Then I'll have to take *The Earl of Zetland* to Aberdeen and look for a job there or in Glasgow,' Adam told him. The steamship *Earl of Zetland* plied between Lerwick and Aberdeen. Adam sounded rather unhappy and Ian guessed why. The chances of a Shetland boy getting a job in the islands were not very great. Most of the islanders had to go south to Scotland or even to England to get jobs.

'What will you do with Haki if you have to go away?' Ian asked.

'My father says he'll have to be sold,' Adam said gloomily 'I wish I could find a job where I could still be with Haki. I tell you, Ian, I will *not* be parted from him if I can help it.'

Ian nodded sympathetically. 'Aye, Adam, he's a grand pony.'

'He's broken in to bridle and saddle now. You'd be surprised at the things he can do,' Adam said with pride. 'Come up the hill-side with me and see him.'

'He's just grand!' Ian declared. 'Will you be showing him at Lerwick, Adam?'

'At the Lerwick Show with the other Shetland ponies, you mean?'

'Yes, the show that's held at the time of the pony sales. That's the week after the school closes.'

At the words 'pony sales' Adam's face darkened.

'I'm sure Haki would take a prize,' Ian said hurriedly. 'Then maybe your father would want to keep him.'

'Well, I might show him,' Adam said thoughtfully 'Will you go with me to the show, Ian?'

'Aye, I'll do that,' Ian told him willingly. 'You'll need to groom him well and teach him to walk round a show-ring.'

'He'll soon learn *that*,' Adam said with confidence.

5

The pony show

Every day Adam spent some time getting Haki ready for the show. He brought Haki down to the stable.

'Have you any old raggy towels?' he asked his mother.

'What do you want them for, Adam?'

'I'm going to give Haki a bath.'

'Mercy me! What next?' Mrs Cromarty exclaimed.

'I want to get him absolutely clean before I start grooming him. I'm thinking I'll maybe put him in for the Lerwick Show.'

'You'll be asking for a bed for that beastie yet,' his mother laughed. All the same she found some old towels and a tattered bed-cover she had been saving for dusters.

Adam got the zinc bath from the back-kitchen and heated water in the kettle which he added to cold water to make the bath lukewarm.

'Can I have a handful of your washing flakes and that old scrubbing brush?' he begged.

'Are you sure you wouldn't like some of those scented bath-cubes from the chemist?' his mother teased him. 'All right! I'll put the bill for the washing flakes alongside the bill for all the sugar you take for that animal.'

Haki was even more surprised than Mrs Cromarty at his bath. He stood there looking miserable while Adam lathered him well, scrubbed him, then rinsed off the soap. The last operation made Haki jump and snort.

'Now to get you dry again!' Adam said.

Haki had his own ideas about getting dry. Just as Adam was taking the towel to him, he shook himself vigorously. Adam received an unexpected shower-bath.

'Stop it, Haki! Stand still!' he cried.

Magnus Cromarty was looking through the kitchen window. He almost doubled up with laughing. Adam looked as if he did not know whether to use the towels for Haki or himself! Magnus went out to the yard as Adam began to towel Haki vigorously.

'Is Friday night to be bath night every week for the two of you?' he laughed. Then he became serious. 'Your mother says you intend to show Haki at Lerwick. It's all right to give him one bath or maybe two before you start grooming him, but don't overdo it and don't give him a bath just before the Show.'

'Why not?' Adam asked.

'Shetland ponies have a kind of oil in their coats which makes them look smooth and shiny. Wash it all out and they'll look woolly like a sheep. You'd lose points on that at a show. Besides, too many baths might give him a chill.'

Adam listened to what his father had to say. He knew Magnus had shown ponies from time to time and taken prizes with them.

'I'll only bath him this once,' he promised. 'Now I've got his mane and tail clean I can easily keep him groomed.'

Magnus went up to the store-room over the stable and returned with a stiff brush and a curry-comb. 'Use these on him well every day, lad.'

Adam spent a lot of time each day grooming Haki's coat and paying special attention to his mane and tail. The little animal looked sleek and shining. He liked the grooming too and came forward when he saw the brush in Adam's hand.

Adam marked out a ring with stones in the pasture. Every day he took Haki by the bridle and walked him round the ring so that he got used to moving easily in a circle. He trained him to trot, too, with his head held straight. Perhaps the hardest thing of all was to train Haki to stand absolutely still, squarely on his four feet, and to allow someone else to approach and lift one of his feet. It was Magnus who suggested this part of the training.

'He must be taught not to back away when the judge comes to get a close look at him. Most likely the judge will want to lift a foot to look at it.'

In turn Magnus Cromarty and Ian Sinclair pretended to be judges and come to look closely at Haki. At first he was shy of them and tried to back. A word from Adam stopped him. After a while he learned to stand still as a rock and let Magnus or

Ian lift any foot and even look in his mouth.

'He's a sweet-tempered, mannerly wee beast,' Mr Cromarty declared. 'He'll behave himself well at the Show. We'd better have shoes put on him, though. A pony that's not shod slips more easily. I'll get old Alexander to fit him out.'

Alexander had once been a blacksmith. Now he ran a small garage in Scalloway, but he still did some smith-work for the farmers. He fitted out Haki with four lightweight shoes. Haki soon got used to them when Adam took him walking and riding along the roads. Haki was ready now for the Show in Lerwick.

'If I walk him seven miles to Lerwick on the day of the Show he'll arrive dusty and tired. I wonder what we could do about it?' Adam consulted Ian.

'Listen! I've got an uncle in Lerwick,' Ian said. 'He's got a farm just at the edge of the town. Maybe he'd let us put Haki in a stable there if we went to Lerwick the night before the Show. We could sleep in the loft above. That would take care of all of us if you don't mind a night on the hay.'

'Suits me!' Adam said promptly. 'That would let me be near Haki all night in case he felt lonely in a strange place.'

Ian brought word from his Uncle Peter that he'd be quite pleased to put up the boys and Haki in his stable and he had sleeping-bags he could lend them.

Adam sent for entry forms from the Show Committee and he and Magnus filled them up. The

Show was to be on the Saturday of the week that Ian and Adam finished school for good.

'I see there's to be a pony sale after the Show,' Magnus remarked. 'What about taking Haki to it?'

Adam felt as if he had had a blow to his heart. 'Why should I? I don't want to sell Haki,' he said rebelliously.

'Now, look here, Adam! Sooner or later you'll *have* to part with Haki. I can't pasture any more ponies on the hillside. I'm needing the grass there for the sheep. Besides, we could be doing with the money from selling the pony.'

'But you gave Haki to me for my own pony! I want to keep him.'

'It's for *you* the money is needed. You've got to find a job, lad, and you'll need to be fitted out with clothes and maybe fares to Aberdeen. You'll need money to pay for lodgings too, till you draw your first pay. *I* can't provide it, Adam. I wish I could, but there's not enough in the bank.'

'Couldn't I get a job at the fishing or the fish-freezing factory in Scalloway?' Adam asked desperately.

'I've inquired of both of them and the answer is "No jobs just now." It's no use, Adam. You'd better look round Lerwick and see if there's any opportunity there while you're up for the Show. And you *must* try to sell Haki afterwards for as good a price as you can get. Seeing he's your pony I'll not come to the sales. I'll leave the selling to you. Then you

64

can choose his new master for yourself, if you get more than one bid for him. But mind, now, Adam, you're to promise me to sell him if you can.'

'I promise,' Adam said unhappily. He knew his father was right. The farm could not support another man or another pony. All the joy seemed to have gone out of preparing Haki for the Lerwick Show.

'A fair price would be thirty-five to forty pounds, seeing Haki's from pedigreed stock,' Magnus instructed. 'It all depends how he does at the Show. But don't refuse any reasonable offer if the colt seems likely to get a good master.'

Adam nodded, his heart too full for speech.

On the Friday before the Show Ian and Adam set out on foot for Lerwick, seven miles away.

'See you come back with a prize, Adam!' his mother called.

'Hold Haki a minute!' Adam said, thrusting the reins into Ian's hands. He rushed back and gave his mother a bear-like hug.

'Good-bye, Mother!' he said.

'Now, what took Adam to do that?' Mrs Cromarty asked Magnus. 'He's no' a lad to wear his heart on his sleeve. You'd think he was going away for good.'

To Adam and Ian a walk of seven miles was nothing. They might have ridden Haki in turn but Adam was very anxious that Haki should not sweat too much. All the weight Haki carried was Adam's bagpipes!

They got a great welcome from Peter Sinclair. He was a big powerful man, fair-haired and blue-eyed, like the Vikings he claimed as ancestors. He shook Adam warmly by the hand and looked Haki over.

'So this is the grand pony Ian mentioned?' Peter Sinclair had once been a breeder of ponies. 'Aye, he's a good colt right enough. You've got him well groomed and in good condition. I'll show you where you can stable him. You can both have a shake-down in the straw store by the stable. Your aunt's got your supper ready, so come into the house,' Uncle Peter said.

'I – I'd like to feed and water Haki first, if you don't mind,' Adam stammered. 'He'll be ready for his supper too.'

'Right, get through with the feeding and by then the wife will have the ham and eggs ready.'

Mrs Sinclair gave them a warm welcome and piled their plates high. After supper the boys stayed talking in the farm kitchen for a while. Ian sounded his uncle about the possibilities of employment for Adam in Lerwick.

'Well, you might get temporary employment during the holiday season when the shops need extra hands, but I'm afraid when the autumn comes you'd be out of a job again, Adam. I'd take you on here for the summer, but in winter I'd have to lay you off again.'

'You don't know anyone who wants a lad *and* a pony, do you?' Adam asked desperately.

Mr Sinclair shook his head. 'Try round at the Employment Exchange office tomorrow on your way to the Show. You might be lucky.'

Next morning they rose to a bright sunny day.

'I'll give you a hand with the grooming, Adam,' Ian said.

Together they went at the little pony with brush and currycomb. Haki stood still, enjoying it. His coat shone like shot-silk. Adam brushed and combed tail and mane till they rippled like waterfalls. Ian polished the harness and saddle till they reflected the sun's rays.

'Haki's just wonderful, Adam. I'm sure he'll take a prize. You ought to get a good price for him at the sale afterwards.'

Adam dropped the brush. 'That's what I'm afraid of – that he will sell. Maybe if he didn't look so beautiful no one would buy him. Then I'd be able to take him back home again.'

'That wouldn't solve your problem,' Ian told him. 'You've *still* got to get a job for yourself and that would part you from Haki anyway.'

'Too true!' Adam said gloomily.

The boys felt very proud as they led Haki through the narrow flagged main street of Lerwick, like a wide pavement on which traffic and pedestrians good-naturedly mingled.

'You hold Haki, Ian,' Adam said, giving him the bridle, when they reached the Employment Exchange.

When Adam came out again he looked troubled.

'Your Uncle Peter was right, Ian. Only jobs for the summer season here and that's half over. If I want a job I can stay in, I'll have to cross the sea.' There was a hint of excitement in Adam's voice all the same. He would not have been a true Shetland lad if the prospect of 'crossing the sea' had not appealed to his spirit of adventure.

They climbed the narrow twisting streets to the field where the Show was to be held. Already people were pouring in through the gates. Besides the classes for animals there were exhibits of agricultural implements, animal foods, and a wonderful display of Shetland knitting, many-coloured scarves, Norse-patterned sweaters, fleecy white shawls. There was a sheep-shearing competition which went on for the greater part of the day.

Adam and Ian made their way to the part of the ground reserved for the animals. The animals were kept in separate pens near the Ring. There were classes for ponies, for cattle, for sheep and sheep-dogs. Among the ponies there were classes for stallions, mares, colts and fillies. Adam had entered Haki in the Colts' Class. The showing of the ponies would not take place till mid-day.

One of the stewards allotted a pen to Haki.

'I'm going to stay here,' Adam told Ian. Haki's well-behaved enough but he's not been used to many other animals. It's his first showing and I don't want him to get excited. You go and have a look at the rest of the Show.'

Ian was back before long with news of the folk he had met round the Show.

'There are one or two good ponies from Unst,' he said. Unst was the northernmost island and famous for its pony breeding. 'All the same, I didn't see any better colts than Haki. I saw my uncle and he says there are buyers here from England.'

Adam did not know whether to be pleased or dismayed by this news. He had half-hoped there might be no buyers. They munched the bread and cheese Mrs Sinclair had put up for them. Adam saw that Haki had a drink of water. The time came to lead him to the show-ring. Adam handed Ian his bagpipes.

'Look after those for me, please, Ian.'

The colts were judged first. Adam had drawn fourth place in the order of showing. He stood at the entrance to the ring, gripping Haki firmly by his bridle. He watched how his competitors fared.

The first pony, a piebald, was shy and nervous. He was led into the ring by his owner. He kicked up his hind legs and refused to follow at a sedate pace. He almost pushed his master round with his nose and there was a gust of laughter from the spectators.

'He wasn't very well-behaved in the ring,' Ian commented.

'No. *We'll* have to do better than that, Haki,'

Adam told his pony. Haki nuzzled his arm as if he understood.

In the excitement of the competition. Adam forgot that soon he might be selling Haki. He was keen now that his animal should do well.

The second pony was more docile and stepped neatly behind his master as he was led round the ring. He was a grey pony in good condition and well groomed.

'He's a good pony,' Adam said. 'I doubt if Haki can beat him.'

'He's too long in the head,' Ian said critically. 'Haki's a better animal.'

The third pony came into the ring. He was a coal-black Shetland with a mane and tail which shone like jet.

'That's a magnificent colt. My father says the judges and the buyers favour black shelties.' Adam gave a regretful sigh.

'Wait and see how he gets on,' Ian said.

The black pony paced round the ring like a proud Arab steed. Next he trotted beautifully, lifting up his little hoofs with precision.

'The prize is as good as his,' Adam said mournfully.

'He's not finished showing yet,' Ian reminded Adam.

At a sign from the judges the exhibitor brought his pony to a standstill. The judge approached to examine his legs and feet. The pony gave him a look out of his eye-corner and backed abruptly. The judge followed him up and put out a hand. The pony shied and lashed out with his legs. It was plain he would not tolerate a stranger handling him.

'That's done it!' Ian whispered exultingly. 'Haki is *far* better behaved than that. He'll stand still all right.'

'My turn now!' Adam said, quaking inwardly. He did his best to control his nervousness lest he should communicate it to Haki.

'You'll be all right. Go in and win!' Ian cheered him on.

Adam moved quietly into the ring, Haki following him on a slack rein. They paused for a moment to gain poise before Adam began to walk round. Haki tossed his mane and looked about him with composure. He held his head well, almost proudly. Though he had not made the dashing entrance of the black colt, he walked easily, neatly, and with confidence.

Haki trotted obediently around the ring with Adam on his back, his head held straight. Adam concentrated all his attention on Haki and Haki quietly obeyed all his commands. A little murmur of admiration and approval ran round the spectators at Adam's perfect, gentle control. One stout, well-dressed man looked specially interested. He was making entries in a notebook.

The judge made a signal to Adam, who slipped off Haki's back. 'Stand still, Haki!' he said.

The little pony immediately stood square, his four feet very correctly placed. He froze into position, like a statue of a pony. The judge approached and put out a hand to Haki's right foreleg to grip the fetlock. To his surprise, Haki lifted his hoof and put the fetlock neatly in the judge's grasp. It was almost as if Haki was shaking hands!

The judge examined Haki's hoof and leg. Haki remained perfectly poised and did not attempt to withdraw his leg. The judge put it down and moved to the next foreleg. Once again Haki lifted it and placed it in friendly fashion in the judge's hand. A murmur of applause came from the crowd.

The judge made an even more thorough examination of the colt. He opened his mouth and looked at his teeth. He looked at Haki's mane and felt at his withers. Haki submitted to the examination with unconcern.

'The judge is giving Haki a right going-over,' Ian whispered to Uncle Peter, who had joined him at the ring-side.

'That's a good sign,' his uncle replied. 'He wouldn't go to so much trouble if the colt was out-classed and not in the running. He's certainly be-having well.'

The stout stranger was underlining Adam's entry in the programme of the show.

At last the judge's examination was over. He signed to Adam that he and the colt could leave the ring. At that precise moment a pipe band at the other side of the field struck up *Scotland the Brave*.

Haki pricked up his ears. He gave Adam a puzzled look. Adam was not playing his bagpipes. All the same that was Adam's tune to which he had learned to march. As Adam led him out his feet fell into a marching rhythm. Haki followed him, stamping his little hoofs in time to the march. The crowd broke into a roar of applause.

'You'd think there was a smirk on that pony's face!' Uncle Peter declared.

Ian rushed to meet Adam.

'Did we do all right?' Adam asked him anxiously.

'Man, you and Haki were just grand! He never put a foot wrong,' Ian declared.

There were several other entries to be judged. The boys waited till the pony show was over. The judges conferred together, comparing their papers. Though they did not really take long, it seemed an age to Adam and Ian. At last the chief judge came forward.

'The prize for the best colt under three years not previously shown at any show is awarded to Adam Cromarty of Scalloway for his colt Haki,' the judge announced. 'This is a fine colt in excellent condition, smart, responsive and exceedingly well-behaved. I should like to offer my congratulations to this lad for the admirable job he has made of training his colt.'

Adam could hardly believe his ears.

'Will Adam Cromarty and his colt Haki please come into the ring to receive his award?'

Adam stood for a moment stupefied at his good

fortune. Ian gave him a nudge. 'Go on, lad! Don't stand there staring! Go and collect your prize!'

Adam came to with a jerk. 'Here! Give me those bagpipes!' In a moment he had the drones sounding. The reins were already looped round Haki's neck. 'Come on, Haki!'

They stepped boldly into the ring. Adam did not even touch Haki's rein, much less lead him. He trusted the little pony to follow him without question. To the triumphant sounds of *Scotland the Brave* Haki marched round the ring to the judge's dais. When they were opposite the chief judge, Adam let the skirl of the pipes die away.

'Stand still, Haki!' he commanded.

Haki stood like a monument, not even turning his head. The judge came forward and attached a blue-and-white rosette to his harness. He turned to Adam, shook hands with him, then presented him with a small silver cup.

'This is yours for a year,' he said. 'It will be inscribed with your name and Haki's at a jeweller's. Inside the cup is your prize.'

Adam and Haki left the ring with the applause ringing in their ears. Ian ran to meet them.

'Here! You take the cup,' Adam said to him. 'I want to get Haki out of this mob. Take care of it. My prize is in the envelope.'

Adam and Ian retreated to the far corner of the field. As soon as they reached it Adam fished three lumps of sugar out of his pocket and gave them to

Haki. 'You've earned these, lad,' he said, stroking Haki between the ears.

'Here! Catch hold of your prize! Don't you want to look at it?' Ian laughed.

Adam tore open the envelope. Inside it was a five-pound note! 'Jings!' he exclaimed. 'I just don't believe it!'

6

What came of the show

Shortly afterwards Uncle Peter crossed the field to join them. With him was the stout stranger who had watched the judging of the Shetland ponies and had made entries in his notebook.

'Well done, Adam! You and Haki put up a wonderful show,' Uncle Peter said. 'This is Mr George Wiggins from England.' There was shaking of hands all round. 'Mr Wiggins is interested in buying Shetland ponies. He has bought them from me in the past.'

Adam's heart gave a thud. So this was it? Had the moment come to sell Haki?

'I'm rather interested in that pony of yours, young man,' Mr Wiggins was saying. 'Mr Sinclair tells me you are thinking of selling him.'

Adam could only nod dumbly.

'Mr Sinclair says the pony belongs to you. Do you mind if I look him over?' Mr Wiggins handled the colt with experienced hands. Haki stood quite still.

'Aye, he's a good sound animal and docile too. Well, my lad, what price are you wanting for him?'

'Well, I – I – ' Adam stammered. He wanted to say, 'I don't wish to sell him,' but he thought of his father and the words would not come. All he could get out was, 'I don't know.'

'I've got a reputation for making a fair deal and I've no intention of doing you down. I'm offering you fifty pounds.'

Adam almost gasped. Fifty pounds! Why that was far more than the price his father had suggested. Still he did not speak.

'Well, Mr Sinclair, do you consider that a fair offer?' Wiggins asked the farmer.

Mr Sinclair did not rush to reply. He wanted to get as good a price as possible for Adam. 'Seeing the animal's a prize-winner, you might make it guineas,' he ventured.

'All right, then, fifty guineas,' Mr Wiggins said rather testily. 'Well, what about it, my lad?'

Suddenly Adam came to. 'If Mr Sinclair thinks fifty guineas is a fair price, then it is. But before I agree to sell Haki I'd like to ask you a few questions, Mr Wiggins.'

'All right! What do you want to know?'

'Will Haki be well treated?'

'Yes, he will indeed.'

'Will he have a good home with *you*?'

Mr Wiggins looked a bit surprised. 'He won't exactly be living with me. I'll be passing him on to someone else to look after, but I shall see him every day. I can assure you he'll be well cared for.'

Adam summoned up courage to ask another question. 'Who will have him, then?'

'Why, the circus, of course!'

'The circus!' It was Adam's turn to look surprised.

'Yes. I thought you knew that I bought animals for my circus.'

'I didn't have the chance to explain to Adam,' Mr Sinclair put in.

'And would Haki be trained for showing in a circus?' Adam asked.

'That's the idea. Circus animals are very well treated indeed. Their training is done by kindness. It's a mistaken idea that they're trained by the whip. You wouldn't get far that way with any animal.'

'I know that,' Adam replied.

'Well, are you willing to sell him?' Mr Wiggins sounded a bit impatient.

A wonderful idea suddenly struck Adam like a blinding light.

'Mr Wiggins. I'll sell him to you if I can go with him. Can you give me a job at the circus too, so that I can be with Haki?'

The others stared at him. 'Oh, come –' Mr Wiggins was beginning.

'Adam's awfully good at training Haki,' Ian broke in. 'He taught Haki how to march behind him when he played the bagpipes.'

Mr Wiggins looked doubtful.

'I've taught Haki other tricks as well,' Adam put in eagerly. 'Watch this!' He turned to Haki. 'Show your hoofs! One!' Haki obediently held up his right forefoot. 'Down!' Haki dropped the foot. 'Two!' Up came the left forefoot! 'Three!' The right hind foot was brought up. 'Four!' Haki showed the left hind foot.

Mr Wiggins was impressed. 'Pretty good! Anything else?' he asked.

'Lie down and go to sleep, Haki!'

Obediently Haki knelt down, rolled over and even shut his eyes!

Adam flicked one of his ears. 'Get up, Haki!' Haki rose to his feet.

'If I'd known he could do all that I would have said his price should be higher,' Peter Sinclair said candidly.

'Of course the trainers at the circus are experienced people,' Mr Wiggins pointed out.

'He's not used to anyone else training him,' Adam put in quickly. 'I could teach him lots more yet.'

'I might be willing to advance my offer to sixty pounds,' Mr Wiggins said.

Adam saw that Mr Wiggins wanted the colt very

much. He turned stubborn and decided to press home his advantage.

'But I want a job, and I want my job to be with Haki. Mr Wiggins, I'd be willing to sell Haki to you for fifty pounds provided you take me on for a year at the circus too, to help to train him.'

'Well, Adam, you'd have to learn the tricks of the trade too. You'd be a kind of apprentice.' Mr Wiggins was weakening. After all, here was a chance to acquire a likely lad too. He decided to take a chance on it.

'I can't offer you big money. You're only a beginner, remember. Will you take fifty pounds for the animal and ten pounds a week pay? You'd have to be responsible for the grooming, exercise and feeding of your animal as well as showing him in the circus ring. *And* you'd have to lend a hand setting up and taking down the circus when we're on the road touring the towns. It's not an easy life.'

'It would suit me all right,' Adam declared. 'I've not been brought up soft.'

'Are you willing to settle for the amount I offered, then?'

There was a streak of caution and foresight in Adam where Haki was concerned. If he sold Haki outright the colt would belong to Mr Wiggins and they could be separated.

'I'll agree if you'll promise to keep me on for twelve months, and if I can have the right to buy back Haki for fifty pounds before or by the end of that time. Oh, and you would have to pay my fare to England because I haven't got any money.'

Mr Wiggins reflected. The circus was a life where one took chances, and after all this was not too big a venture. He had taken bigger chances with elephants and their trainers. If at the end of twelve months Adam was not suited to the circus, at least they'd have his services as a groom and a handyman. As for the promise to redeem his pony, one need not take that too seriously. Once a lad earned money, he soon spent it too. He couldn't see Adam saving up fifty pounds even in a year, and even if he did pay it back, they would have had the animal's services for nothing for a year. It was not too bad a bargain.

'Very well,' Mr Wiggins said at last. 'I'll agree. Fifty pounds down for Haki. You join the circus at ten pounds a week with the option of buying back your animal at what I gave for it within the next twelve months. It's a deal.'

'It's a deal,' Adam agreed. 'Will you please put it in writing for Mr Sinclair here to witness it?'

'Well, my word is my bond, as Mr Sinclair will tell you, but come back with me to my hotel and we'll put it in writing. For a lad who's making his first business deal, you know what you're about.'

They followed Mr Wiggins to his hotel in the centre of the town. Ian held on to Haki while Adam and the two men went up to the lounge. There, on a big table under the window, Mr Wiggins wrote out the agreement.

They both signed it, Mr Sinclair as witness, then

Mr Wiggins handed it to Adam. 'There you are. You keep that. And now, you must have the pony ready down at the wharf to sail at five p.m. on the steamship.'

Adam had not realized they would leave so soon. There would be no time to go home to Scalloway and make the journey back again! No time for farewells! Adam was at the crossroads of his life. He hesitated.

'I did not know you would be going so soon. There will be no time for me to go home to tell my parents.'

'There's no Sunday boat, so I must leave Shetland tonight to get to my circus. I can't afford to waste time here. Come on, boy! You must make up your mind.'

Adam thought quickly. Sooner or later he would have to seek a job across the sea. This was the only job where he could be with Haki. Indeed, his job would *be* Haki! His father had told him he must sell the pony. He would go with him.

'I'll come with you, Mr Wiggins.'

'Good!' Mr Wiggins was pleased at Adam's quick decision. The circus had no room for wafflers. 'Here is your fifty pounds.' Mr Wiggins counted it out in five-pound notes. 'Look out for me at the quay at half past four. I'll expect you to have the animal aboard by then.'

'I'll do that,' Adam promised.

Adam felt a bit dazed when he rejoined Ian in the street.

'I've got to sail on the five o'clock boat!'

'Well, that's quick work! Are you sure your father won't be mad?' Ian asked.

'I've only done what he told me: sold the pony and got myself a job. Ian, will you go to my father and tell him what's happened?'

'Aye, I'll do that.'

'And will you give him the money for Haki?' Adam thrust the envelope containing the fifty pounds into Ian's hands.

'I'll take it straight to him on my way home. Any other messages?'

'Yes. Tell – tell my mother I'll write to her.' Adam's voice began to choke. 'Tell her I'll *aye* be writing every week and sending money to her.'

'Adam, should you not keep back part of Haki's price? You'll need clothes, and things like soap.'

'I've still got Haki's prize money. I can manage on that till I draw my first pay. I'll see what clothes I need when I get to the circus. If I'm only to be mucking out stables and grooming, I'll no' be needing smart clothes.'

Mr Sinclair shook hands with Adam. 'Well, good luck, Adam! Keep up with your piping. You've got the makings of a good piper. The best of luck! See you later, Ian!'

The boys went to the offices of the steamship company.

'Aye, we were told to expect you,' the clerk said. He made out a document and stamped it. 'Take this along to the ship. It's the *Saint Rognvald* lying at the Victoria Pier. Ask for the purser and he'll send a man to show you where the pony is to be berthed.'

Already cargo was being loaded into the ship when they arrived. Adam went to seek the purser while Ian held Haki. He came back with a friendly seaman who said, 'We can take your pony aboard now, son. Just bring him along to the gangway.'

A door in the hull of the ship was open and a gangway was laid from it to the quay.

'Come on, Haki!' Adam gave a gentle tug to the bridle. Haki hesitated and eyed the gangway and the water below it with suspicion. He was not very willing to tread on this strange contraption.

'Come on!' Adam gave a tug to the reins. Haki tried to back away.

Adam slackened his hold on the rein. 'Very well!' he told Haki. 'You can do what you like. *I'm* going aboard.'

Haki watched Adam step on the gangway. Adam did not look back at him. He just strode straight ahead. Haki was seized by a panic lest Adam should go away and leave him behind. He hardly needed Ian's slap on his flanks. He gave one look at Adam's back and obediently trotted up the gangway after him. Another stride or two and he was aboard the ship!

The seaman led them along a passage to a number of stable-like pens, each big enough to take one animal. 'This is yours,' he told Adam.

It was a clean well-ventilated pen with straw bedding.

'See your pony bedded down, then if you go up that companionway at the end of the passage' – he pointed to some stairs – 'you'll find a steward who'll show you to your cabin.'

'Cabin?' Adam was surprised. 'Can't I stay here with my pony?'

The seaman looked astonished. 'Stay if you like, but you'll not find it very comfortable. You'd be better in your cabin. You could keep coming down to look at him.'

'I'll see him settled first and give him a feed,' Adam decided.

Ian looked at his watch. 'It's nearly four o'clock, Adam. D'you mind if I slip into the town for a few minutes? I've got to go to a shop?'

'Right! I'll stay here with Haki.'

It was not long before Ian was back with an armful of small parcels.

'I've brought you some chocolate. There's not been much time for a meal today. And here's half a pound of sugar for Haki and some apples.'

'That's mighty kind of you, Ian!'

'Oh, and here's something I thought you might need,' Ian said awkwardly.

Adam unwrapped it. It was a small plastic writing case containing a writing pad and envelopes and a ballpoint pen. Adam knew it must have taken most of Ian's pocket-money.

'Just so you could write to your folks, you know! I

knew you wouldn't be carrying writing materials around,' Ian excused his own generosity. 'I stuck a wee book of stamps inside too. It's not always easy to get stamps just when you want them.'

'Ian, I – I – thanks a lot!' Adam stammered. 'I – I've got nothing to give you in return.'

'Och, forget it! Just be sending me a line now and again.'

'I'll do that. Listen, Ian! Will you keep my little silver cup? I don't want to take it with me.'

'Right, I will, Adam. Let me know how Haki's getting on at the circus and I'll let you know that your silver cup is being polished.'

A couple of other ponies had come in to the next pens. Haki watched them suspiciously, keeping well to the faraway side of his own pen.

'Haki's going to have to get used to a lot of different animals,' Adam said thoughtfully.

'Aye, and in a circus there'll be some awful strange-like beasts,' Ian remarked. When he saw Adam's look of misgiving he added hastily, 'But Haki's a well-behaved pony. He'll soon learn to get on with them.'

'I hope so,' Adam said doubtfully, conjuring up pictures of lions, tigers, and elephants.

Ian looked at his watch. 'It's coming up towards five o'clock, Adam. Maybe I'd better go on deck to be ready to go down the gangway.'

'I'll come with you to the rail,' Adam said heavily.

Haki whinnied after them as they went towards the companionway.

'It's all right, Haki. I'm coming back,' Adam told him. Ian turned back to Haki and stroked his head. He could not trust himself to speak. He followed Adam sadly up the stair.

At the gangway Ian turned, 'Well, it's good-bye now, Adam. It'll seem queer in Scalloway this summer without you. You'll mind and write now.'

'Aye, you can count on that.'

The two boys shook hands quickly.

'So long, Adam!'

'So long, Ian!'

The brief farewell hid their feelings. Once on the quay Ian turned and waved and Adam waved back. Adam watched Mr Wiggins coming towards the gangway; then he went below to Haki again.

A few minutes later the ship's siren sounded the warning for all who were not passengers to go ashore. Haki started a little at the sound, but Adam's hand at his shoulder soothed him. The ship's motors began throbbing. Haki turned his head and looked at Adam.

'It's all right, Haki. Lie down!'

Obediently the colt settled down in the straw. Adam sat down beside him. Once again the siren sounded. The gangways were hoisted. The motors increased their throbbing. Bells rang on the bridge.

Slowly the *Saint Rognvald* moved from the

quayside into the Sound of Bressay. It was a quiet evening. The wind that so often blows in Shetland was just a gentle breeze. The sea rippled peacefully. Only the sea-birds wheeled and screamed.

Haki grew used to the throb of the engines and relaxed in the straw. Adam gave him an apple and he munched it sleepily. He seemed lulled by the movement of the ship. Adam rose to his feet.

'I'll be back soon, Haki,' he said.

The colt raised his head to watch him leave the pen, then lazily settled down to sleep. It had been a long, exciting day for him and he was glad now to be undisturbed.

Adam went on deck. The Sound was widening out now to the North Sea. Lerwick had dwindled to a mass of roof-tops astern. For a short time the ship kept parallel with the coast, then she gradually altered course towards the south-east. Adam leaned on the rail and watched the land recede, his heart heavy, his mind a turmoil of thoughts. He looked at the little white-washed crofts, so like his own home. The Isle of Mousa merged with the mainland. The coast looked misty, dream-like, as though seen through a veil. The lace-like waves curled whitely round the feet of the great grey cliffs. It seemed as though the land was moving, wheeling away, and not the ship.

Adam watched the coast dwindle till it was a ragged black line of cliffs topped by the greens and browns of the moorland, a blur of pastel colours on the deeper blue of the sea.

'Good-bye, Shetland!' His lips framed the words silently. 'Will I ever be back?'

For a moment he stood there, thinking of the croft below the hills above Scalloway; of Hecla, busy now with the next foal that was not his to train; of his father tending the sheep; of his mother knitting away patiently, knitting in every spare moment that poverty might not knock at their door. At the thought of her kind quiet face, the warm tears gushed into his eyes. He walked resolutely forward and stared at the far, mysterious horizon behind which lay his destination and his future.

Adam was following the path that so many sons of Shetland had had to take, ever since remembered time. To live and prosper they had to leave the islands. In all the countries of the world were Shetland's exiled children. Adam's thoughts were those of the lads who for centuries had left the islands. There was one difference, though. Adam was taking Haki with him. With Haki was comfort and love. Adam turned away from the ship's rail and went below to the little pony.

7

Arrival at the circus

It was quite a comfortable voyage. Haki settled down well, contented that Adam was near him, and Adam shared his chocolate and apples with the colt. Before he went to his cabin, though, he ran up on deck to see if he could still see the islands. They had vanished in the deep blue haze of the northern night. There was only the deeper blue of the sea around them. There was a smell of cigar smoke. Adam turned and saw Mr Wiggins at the rail.

'Taking a breather before you turn in? I didn't see you at supper in the saloon,' Mr Wiggins remarked.

'I had mine beside Haki – the pony, you know. I didn't want him to feel strange.'

'Very fond of that animal, aren't you, boy?'

'Yes, Mr Wiggins.'

'That's a good thing. A circus trainer needs to be on good terms with his animals. Now see your pony's fed and watered and then get to your bed. I've no use for half-awake lads in the morning.'

Adam felt comforted by what Mr Wiggins had said. He slipped down to Haki. The little colt sleepily opened one eye, looked at Adam, then settled down again.

'I think it's going to be all right, Haki,' Adam

whispered. 'We'll both have to work hard and we'll have to stick out lots of strange things, but we'll get by.'

Adam was astonished at the comfort of his cabin, his bunk with a soft mattress, snowy white pillows and sheets. There was even a hand-basin with hot and cold water; Adam peeled off his jacket and turned on the hot-water tap. After a good wash he settled into his bunk. He hardly seemed to have been asleep an hour when there was a tapping at the cabin door. He struggled back to consciousness and sat up.

'Yes. What is it?'

The door opened. It was a steward with a tray in his hand.

'Here's your morning tea, laddie.'

'My morning tea!' Adam goggled at him. 'Guid sakes! What time is it?'

'It's six o'clock and we're drawing in to Aberdeen.'

'Aberdeen? My goodness, I must have been asleep for hours!'

Adam wasted no time in drinking his tea, dressing and going down to Haki's quarters. Haki was just struggling to his feet and shaking himself. He looked round in a bewildered fashion. He had had a very comfortable bed among the straw.

'Hullo, Haki! You're not used to all this luxury either, are you?' Adam laughed. 'It's a bit different from a Shetland hillside with a snell wind blowing.' Adam felt a pang of homesickness for the rough moorland and the bracing Shetland wind. He buried his face in Haki's shoulder. Haki seemed to know Adam was sad for he turned and licked his hands and face.

He groomed Haki, watered and fed him, then went in search of his own breakfast. Mr Wiggins was already seated with bacon and eggs before him.

'Your pony ready, Adam?'

'Aye, sir. He only needs to have halter and bridle on.'

'Good! Make a good breakfast yourself.'

After breakfast Adam went on deck. Aberdeen was appearing on the sky-line. In the early morning sun the granite buildings sparkled and shone. They rose, one behind another on the low hill. Among them soared the spires of many churches. Adam's eyes grew wide. 'Why, Aberdeen's bigger than Lerwick!' he exclaimed. To the Shetland boy Lerwick had always seemed one of the largest cities in the world.

The ship steamed its way up the estuary to Matthew's Quay. As the ship eased into its berth Adam went down to Haki. He put on his halter and bridle. Haki licked him affectionately. A seaman came along the line of pens and said, 'We're ready to discharge the animals now. You can lead your pony out.'

Adam led Haki out to the gangway. The pony looked dubiously again at the sloping contraption with the glint of sea-water below it, but Adam said firmly, 'Come on, Haki!' and gave a little tug to the bridle. He took the pony slowly down to the concrete quay. Once on firm ground Haki shook himself vigorously as if thankful he had made the passage from ship to shore without mishap.

Mr Wiggins was already on the quay, smoking his cigar. He looked Haki over with approval.

'Good lad! You've groomed him already. Now wait here till we get the other animals ashore.'

'The other animals?' Adam was surprised.

'Yes. The other Shetland ponies. I bought two more besides Haki.'

'Are they all going to the circus?' Adam asked.

'Yes. These two will draw a carriage for the chimps.'

'Chimps?'

'Yes. Chimpanzees. Monkeys, you know.'

'Oh!' Adam was astonished. 'And will Haki—?'

Mr Wiggins understood the question before Adam finished it. 'No we shan't mix Haki with the chimps. He ought to make a turn on his own, though we might team him up with some other animal later.'

'Where is the circus just now?' Adam asked.

'Oh, we're at Edinburgh. It's our tenting season just now.'

'Tenting?'

'Aye, tenting is what circus people call it when they go on tour. My folk'll be setting up the circus today at Murrayfield. That's on the west side of Edinburgh. Performances start tomorrow.'

Mr Wiggins laughed at the troubled look on Adam's face.

'It's all right Adam. We shan't start showing Haki till he's got used to the bustle of the circus. We'll give him time to settle down and learn his act first. It wouldn't pay us to push an untrained animal into the ring. You'll both be put through your paces. Ah, here come the other ponies! Once they're landed we can get them all into the horse-box.' Mr Wiggins pointed to a large van that was standing near the end of the quay. On its side was painted in bright red letters 'George Wiggins' Circus'.

'It's one of our own vans come up to meet the ship. I phoned for it before we left Shetland. You didn't think we were going to ride the ponies all the way to Edinburgh, did you?' Mr Wiggins's laugh echoed round the harbour.

A man swung down from the van and approached them. He wore riding breeches and a polo-necked sweater.

'Morning, Mr Wiggins!' he said cheerfully. 'Picked up some bargains?' He looked inquiringly at Adam.

'Hullo, Jake! I've picked up a future performer as well.' Mr Wiggins said with a grin. 'Meet Adam Cromarty. He's going to join us with his pony Haki. This is Jake Bradley, Adam. Jake's in charge of our horses and ponies.'

Jake held out his hand. 'What's your line, Adam?'

Adam looked perplexed. Mr Wiggins spoke for him.

'Oh, he'll do an act with Haki later on when we've rehearsed him a bit. He'll play the bag-pipes.'

'Bagpipes! We've never had a piper before.'

'He's quite good with them. The other ponies are ready now. We'll get them into the horse-box.'

Adam looked at the other two Shetland ponies. They were skewbald ponies, brown and cream, pretty enough, but not in the same class as Haki for appearance. Jake took them over and Adam led Haki to the horse-box. He was relieved to find it was divided into separate stalls.

Jake called to Adam. 'Bring your pony up now.'

Adam went first up the ramp, holding the bridle loosely. Haki only hesitated for one brief second. Where Adam led, Haki would always follow.

'You can hitch him up in the stall nearest our seat at the front,' Jake told Adam. He pointed to a little shutter which was open between the driver's seat and the interior of the horse-box. 'You'll be sitting in front with me and Mr Wiggins. You can keep taking a peep through there at your pony and speak to him if he seems a bit restless.'

Adam was grateful to Jake for understanding how he felt about Haki. He tethered Haki and gave him the last of the apples, rubbed his shoulder and said, 'You'll be all right, Haki. I'll not be far away.'

Jake saw the other two ponies into the van, then he and Adam lifted the ramp in place and secured it with cross-bars.

'Now we can be off as soon as Mr Wiggins joins us. Climb up into the driving seat, Adam,' Jake said.

Adam heard an inquiring neigh come from the dark interior of the horse-box. He looked through the aperture and called, 'Quiet now, Haki! Everything's all right.'

Haki was so surprised to hear his voice without seeing Adam that he stared all round him. Adam laughed. The laugh reassured Haki. He gave a grumbling little whinny and settled down. Mr Wiggins joined them and soon they were speeding through Aberdeen. Adam stared open-mouthed at the big shops with their plate-glass windows. They crossed a bridge over the River Dee.

'I've never seen such a wide river!' Adam exclaimed.

'Have you no rivers in Shetland, Adam?' Jake asked.

'Only small ones, just streams.'

'Wait till you cross the Tay and the Forth then.'

Soon Aberdeen was left behind and they rattled southward. Mr Wiggins fell asleep with his head in the corner of the cab.

Through Perth they went, the road passing through wide park-like spaces, then, once again they left the town behind.

For all his interest in this new and exciting countryside Adam did not forget to keep looking through the opening behind him at Haki. Once or twice the colt seemed restless and pawed with his foot at the floor of the van Adam spoke or whistled to him and Haki settled down again. The motion of the van lulled him and he dozed on his feet.

'You're coming to the Forth Bridge now,' Jake told Adam.

Adam looked at the high towers and the filigree lines of the suspension rods carrying the broad bridge with its four traffic lanes. It seemed such a delicate structure to carry all that weight. This would indeed be something to tell Ian and his parents in his letters. They entered the bridge and Adam looked at the prospect on either side; the sturdy cat's cradle of red iron girders that made the old railway bridge to the east; the widening basin of the Forth above the road bridge.

Mr Wiggins stirred and yawned. 'Ah! Coming towards Edinburgh?' he remarked with satisfaction.

They passed through suburbs of pleasant houses and tree-lined roads. 'You're coming to Princes Street. That's Edinburgh Castle,' Jake pointed out.

Adam was excited. He had heard about Edinburgh Castle at school. The castle rose on high rocks above the town, looking like one out of a legend, silhouetted against the pale blue sky.

'I never thought yesterday that I'd be seeing Edinburgh Castle today,' Adam said.

'Well, take a good look at it now, for once you reach the circus there'll be no time for sight-seeing,' Jake told him. 'It'll be all hands to the job then.'

A little further along the road Mr Wiggins stared ahead. 'Ah! they've got the Big Top up,' he said with satisfaction.

Over the roofs and trees the high-domed top of the circus marquee rose, its flag fluttering bravely in the westerly breeze.

'Aye, we'll be rehearsing the horses this afternoon,' Jake said.

'Rehearsing the horses?' Adam asked.

'Yes, the liberty horses, y'know. We give them the chance to get the feel of the ring in a new place before they give a performance.'

'What are liberty horses?' Adam inquired.

'They're the ones that run round the ring freely and turn when the trainer cracks his whip as a signal. The equestrians leap on and off them and turn somersaults over their backs. My missus does a grand act at it,' Jake said with pride.

'Does your missus perform in the circus?' Adam was surprised.

'Oh, aye! Everybody has to do something in a circus. That's right, isn't it, Mr Wiggins? Even your daughters.'

'Aye, the girls don't do badly on the high-wire,' Mr Wiggins said.

'The high-wire?' Adam was feeling bewildered by this new world of the circus.

'They walk and dance on it, high up in the dome

of the Big Top. You'll see it, though. We'll give you a chance to see all the turns before you and the pony take part in the programme.'

Jake took a sharp turn to the left. 'Here we are!' he said.

Adam looked about him with keen interest. Beyond the Big Top were the animals' quarters, connected to the show tent by a long canvas-covered passage. Jake came to a stop.

'This is where the horses are stabled, there at the far end. The lions are in a cage nearest the ring, and the chimps are between them and the horses.'

Behind the animals' quarters, in the far side of the field, were the gay-coloured caravans and small tents of the circus people.

Mr Wiggins swung off the van. 'Get the ponies stabled, Jake. Then will you look after Adam and see that he gets a meal? I'm away to the Big Top to see what's going on there.'

'Don't forget your own dinner, Mr Wiggins, or Mrs Wiggins will be on your track,' Jake said, chuckling. He turned to Adam. 'Come on and help me to get the ramp down and the ponies out.'

Jake Bradley took out the two Shetland ponies and Adam led out Haki. At the top of the ramp Haki stopped. He stared at the circus scene, sniffed the air and got the scent of the lions. An inherited instinct of fear which went back to some far remote ancestor possessed him. He trembled and neighed violently. An answering roar came from the lions' quarters. Adam felt nervous himself, but he soothed

Haki, saying, 'Now, calm down, Haki. It's going to be all right.' Together they walked down the ramp and into the new world of the circus.

The quarters assigned to the horses were separate from those of other animals. To put lions and bears near to horses would have excited both. Though they got used to each others' scents as they worked in the circus, old fears of the hunted for the hunter were still their inheritance. In the circus they learned to tolerate each other, but never to mingle.

Each pony had a separate stall of iron rails and stout canvas.

'Hitch Haki to the rail and then we'll go and find some dinner,' Jake said.

Adam hesitated. 'I – I'd rather see him settled down first.'

'Now listen, Adam! You can't live, eat and sleep with that animal for ever. It just isn't possible! That way the pony will never settle on his own. He's got to learn independence the same way you're doing by leaving your home and joining the circus.'

'I hadn't thought of that,' Adam said seriously.

'The first thing he's got to learn is when you say, "Bye, bye, Haki, I'll be back," that you *will* come back. He's to learn to trust you when you're *not* there as well as when you're beside him. Now I've got to see the chap who'll be training the other Shetland ponies, so I'll give you a quarter of an hour with Haki. Then say your piece to him, leave him, and meet me at the entrance to the stables.'

Adam fondled Haki and talked to him. He hitched the bridle to the rail and Haki seemed to accept his stall. Adam found he still had ten minutes left of his allotted time so he thought he would try an experiment. He still had a few lumps of sugar left in his pocket. He took one out and held it on the palm of his hand so Haki could see it.

'Bye, bye, Haki! I'll be back,' he said firmly and gave Haki the sugar. Adam strode out of the stall and walked away along the line of the stables. When he got to the end he stood still and listened. There was no sound at first from Haki, then came a protesting neigh. Adam waited a few minutes, then went back to Haki. Haki was pulling at the bridle securing him. Adam pretended to be angry. He scolded Haki and said, 'Keep still, Haki!'

Haki was astonished, but obeyed. It had never happened before that Adam had spoken to him angrily. As soon as he had ceased his restless movements, Adam rewarded him with another piece of sugar. He repeated, 'Bye, bye, Haki! I'll be back!' and disappeared from the stables. Another whinny followed him but this time it was not so indignant and plaintive. Adam waited a minute or two and then returned. This time, though Haki was glad to see him again, he was neither tugging at the rail nor pawing the floor. Twice more Adam repeated the drill. Each time he left him he gave him a lump of sugar and repeated the same words. Each time

Haki seemed more reconciled to his departure. When he gave his little whinny now it was as if he said 'Bye, bye!' too. When Adam finally went through the drill he met Jake outside, Haki made no fuss at all.

'Come along to my living-wagon,' Jake said. 'Ella is expecting you for a meal.'

When they reached the caravan Mrs Bradley was already at the door, Jake made the introductions. She shook Adam warmly by the hand.

'Come in! I've had your dinner in the stove a while.' There was a good smell of cooking.

Adam was surprised how comfortable and well-furnished the caravan was. The bunks were folded into settees. There were lace curtains at the windows. There was even a crystal vase of flowers on the table which was set for three, with place-mats and shining cutlery. Adam could not keep his astonishment out of his face. Mrs Bradley laughed at him.

'You hadn't expected our living-wagon to be as small as this, had you?'

'It – it wasn't that, Mrs Bradley. I had no idea a caravan could be so beautiful.'

Mrs Bradley was pleased.

'It's our home, you see, Adam, and I like to keep it nice for Jake.' She smiled affectionately at her husband. 'But we don't call it a caravan. That makes us sound like gipsies. Circus folk call them "living-wagons".'

'I'll remember,' Adam said.

She began dishing up the dinner. There was a good joint of roast beef, baked potatoes, Yorkshire pudding and a big cauliflower. 'Get busy on the carving, Jake,' she directed him.

A generous heaped-up plate was handed to Adam.

'Get round that, lad. It's a long time since breakfast,' Jake told him.

Adam ate with relish. 'That was just grand,' he said, as he cleaned up the plate. 'I've never eaten Yorkshire pudding before.'

'Never eaten Yorkshire pudding!' Ella Bradley looked at him incredulously. 'Whatever do you eat in those far-off islands you come from?'

'Pease brose and cock-a-leekie and bursten broonies,' Adam said with a twinkle in his eye.

'Mercy on us! What outlandish stuff is that?'

Adam explained in detail.

'Well, it doesn't sound so bad the way you describe it. You can try your hand at the cock-a-leekie on my stove some day and let us taste it,' Ella said.

'Now, Ella, you know quite well it wouldn't be a Sunday for you if you didn't have Yorkshire pudding,' Jake teased her. 'The missus is a right Yorkshire tyke, Adam. Born and bred in Leeds she was!'

The meat course was followed by an excellent apple pie with custard. At last they all sat back from the table, comfortably replete.

'That was a fine dinner. Thank you very much,' Adam told Ella with real appreciation.

'Glad you enjoyed it, luv!' she said, giving him the usual north country term of endearment between friends. 'I'll just side the dishes away while you and Jake have a nap, then we'll have a cup of tea.'

Jake pulled out his pipe but Adam rose and helped Mrs Bradley to carry the dishes to the sink. When she began to wash up, Adam, said, 'Where's a drying towel? I always gave my mother a hand.' He gulped a little over the last remark and Ella gave him a searching glance.

'Is this the first time you've been away from Shetland, Adam?'

'Aye.'

'It – it must feel a bit queer-like –'

'Yes. This time last week I didn't – didn't think –' Adam felt a sudden constriction of homesickness at his throat. 'I – I had to come away without saying good-bye,' he gulped. 'You see, I couldn't let Haki go alone.'

'Haki?'

'Haki's his pony,' Jake explained.

As an equestrienne Ella Bradley had learned to love her horses too and she could understand Adam's love for his pony.

'Poor lad!' she said, laying a hand sympathetically upon his arm. 'Now, don't say another word till the tea's mashed. The kettle's just coming to the boil. Nothing like a cup of tea to raise your spirits!'

While they were drinking the tea Ella asked,

'Did the Boss – Mr Wiggins, you know – tell you where you were to live in the circus?'

'No, he didn't say. I – I thought maybe I'd have to sleep alongside Haki.'

'We do have to rough it sometimes in the circus but we don't doss down with the animals yet,' Jake laughed. 'No, the Boss wouldn't want you to do that unless your animal was ill and had to be watched. He'll be expecting you to get a lodging in a wagon with some of the other lads, no doubt.'

'Perhaps I'd better go and ask him?'

Ella Bradley gave him a little push back on to the settee.

'The Boss would not thank you to disturb his nap just now.'

'Actually he thought Adam might get fixed up in the Baxter Boys' wagon,' Jake said.

'The Baxter Boys!' Ella pulled a face in contempt. 'Oh, I know there's only two of them in that living-wagon but I never saw such a place. If it had been stirred with a soup spoon it couldn't look worse. Heaven knows when those types last cleaned it out! And every night they're down at a pub. Adam's not the kind to muck in with that lot.'

'You've got a point there,' Jake admitted with a grin. He and Ella exchanged a long look and nodded to each other.

'D'you know what I'm thinking, Jake Bradley?' she asked in a challenging tone.

'Most likely what I'm thinking, Mrs Bradley,' Jake chuckled. 'Though, knowing you, you'd talk me round even if I didn't agree. Go ahead!'

Adam looked from one to the other bewildered by this exchange.

'Adam, could you fancy living with us?' Ella asked.

'Oh, yes!' Adam said eagerly and then stopped short. 'But where – er – how?' He looked round the living-wagon. There were only two bunks.'

'No, no, we're not expecting you to sleep on the floor, lad!' Mrs Bradley laughed. 'We've got a little tent we can set up alongside the wagon.'

'There are one or two camp beds in the circus stores. I could draw one out for you,' Jake suggested. 'How would that suit you, Adam?'

'Just fine!' Adam said, his heart full of gratitude.

'You could have your meals here in the wagon with us. Mind you, you won't get roast beef and Yorkshire pudding every day of the week,' Ella warned him. 'I've got my jobs to do in the circus too.'

'Aye, lad it'll be "Nip, scratch and bite" most days except Sundays,' Jake teased.

'Er – er – please, how much would I need to pay for my food and lodging?' Adam asked politely. He had no idea what Ella might ask of him and he *must* set aside something out of his weekly wage to buy Haki back again.

'Oh, two or three pounds, maybe. I'll tell you what I'll do, Adam. I'll see how much all our food costs for a week and divide it by three. Don't worry! I shan't bankrupt you, luv. How's that?'

'It suits me fine,' Adam said happily.

On this light note of mutual trust the bargain was completed.

8

Circus début

When they had finished tea Jake said, 'I'll just be stepping along to the tent and see what's doing there. Coming, Adam?'

'I'll see you later when I come along to do my trick,' Ella told them.

'We'll pick up Haki on the way,' Jake said as they crossed the turf. 'Mr Wiggins said you were to bring your bagpipes too.'

'But Haki won't be expected to – to –' Adam faltered.

'To do his stuff? Not yet. The first part of his training, though, is to get used to the sight and smell of other animals. It's a good chance for you to stand with him in one of the aisles to the seats and let him watch. You'd be surprised what one animal can learn from another.'

Haki welcomed Adam back again with a little nickering sound and nuzzled his arm. He did not seem upset at being left on his own, though there was an indentation in the turf where he had been pawing with one foot. Adam led him along to the Big Top.

'Just take him to that wide aisle over there. That's where the public generally come in. Of course, there won't be any today, being Sunday. It's just a rehearsal for the elephant and horses. The animals enter from the opposite side, so you'll be out of the way there,' Jake instructed him.

Jake stood by him for a minute or two watching the elephant being put through her drill, moving this way and that at a sign from her trainer.

'That's Sonda. She's a very intelligent beast and as gentle as a lamb. Watch her! Bill Crockett is a wonderful trainer.'

At a motion of Bill's stick Sonda rose on her hind legs and waltzed obediently, putting her big feet down with delicate precision. When Bill said 'up!' she lifted him on to her back. At the word 'Down!' she set him gently on the ground again, then stepped right over him, not even disturbing a hair of his head.

Adam thought Haki might have been frightened at the sight of the great beast but he merely seemed curious. Indeed he took a step forward. Sonda had finished her act and was just about to be led away by Bill when she saw Haki. She stood stock-still for a moment, then lifted up her trunk and trumpeted.

Haki was not afraid. In his turn he gave a gentle whinny.

'Michty me!' Adam exclaimed. 'That's Haki's *friendly* call. You'd think he was answering Sonda.'

'Aye, you would,' Jake agreed. 'Strange that! Or is it? Sonda was right fond of a Shetland pony, Gipsy, years ago. She used to do a turn in the ring with him. She was real unhappy when he died. Bill had quite a job to get her to eat. Elephants have very deep feelings, you know.'

'What did the pony die of?' Adam felt a cold fear at his heart lest anything might befall Haki. 'Was it an accident?'

'Bless you, no! It was old age. Gipsy was getting on even when Sonda joined the circus. But they were friends right from the start.'

'It seems funny that they would make friends,' Adam commented.

'Oh, they have their likes and dislikes, just as human beings do. Heaven help any circus man, though, if an elephant takes a dislike to him! Here come the Shetland ponies we brought over with Haki last night.'

'Surely they're not going to perform tomorrow?' Adam asked.

'Oh, no! Not yet. Not till they've got used to pulling a load of chimpanzees round the ring. Willie Baxter is just trying them harnessed to the cart and making a round or two of the ring.'

Willie Baxter led the ponies and cart round the

ring. He had a whip. Though he did not use it on the animals he cracked it rather alarmingly. Haki started and backed a pace or two.

'Go easy! No need to handle the whip quite so much,' Jake Bradley said.

For a turn or two Willie Baxter forbore to crack his whip, but he scowled at Jake and included Adam. Jake noticed the look.

'You can take the ponies out now.'

Willie gave a final crack of his whip which sent the long lash curling wickedly almost to Adam's feet. Adam stood his ground and held on tightly to Haki.

'That's enough, Willie!' Jake said sharply.

Willie drove his animals out of the ring.

'I'll have a word with that young man later,' Jake said with annoyance.

'Why did he flick his whip at *me*?' Adam asked. 'I've never even spoken to him.'

'He's vexed that he's not got the handling of your pony too. He thinks he should have control of all the Shetlands.'

'But Mr. Wiggins took me on specially to look after Haki and to do our turn together,' Adam said, bewildered.

'Oh, aye, lad. Never worry! It's only a bit of spite and showing off. He'll get over it. Just you stand your ground with Willie, that's all. Here come the liberty horses now.'

Music was played from a tape recorder.

Adam drew in his breath with admiration. The

horses came cantering in, each one in step with the others. They were beautiful Arab horses, four chestnuts and four greys, a chestnut alternating with a grey as they flowed round the ring. They tossed their heads proudly as if they knew they were beauties.

Jake advanced into the ring. He held a short whip called a guider. He gave it a little crack and the horses immediately turned and cantered in the opposite direction. They made one or two circuits, turning as Jake gave the signal. Never once did they falter or get out of step. Jake whistled, and twiddled his guider as if stirring porridge. The animals began circling in twos, head to tail, as though waltzing, a chestnut horse with a grey. Adam watched them fascinated. Even Haki peered with bright eyes under his mane. Another crack of the whip and they cantered round the ring again.

Jake cracked his whip twice and the horses separated, the chestnuts going round one way and the greys in the opposite direction. As if going through a country dance the animals threaded in and out of each other's lines. The second time round they fell into their original positions.

Ella appeared in the ring in black practising tights. She leaped and landed like a piece of thistle-down on the leading horse. She stood swaying gently to the movement, then did a gay pirouette which ended in a perfect somersault off the horse's back. The horse never changed his pace but moved steadily round. Before the third horse passed her,

Ella leaped again. This time she did a hand-stand turned it into a back somersault over the head of the fourth horse and landed in a standing position on his back. She rode triumphantly round the ring with one arm upraised as if to acknowledge the applause of a crowd.

Adam watched her fascinated.

'O.K., Ella?' Jake called.

'O.K. The ring's all yours. You might tell Bert to put some more rosin on Sultan's back tomorrow, though. My feet didn't grip too well.'

She leaped down into the ring again. The horses made a concerted bow and cantered out.

Jake crossed over to Adam and Haki. 'Bring Haki in now, Adam, and lead him round the ring once or twice.'

Adam tugged gently at the bridle. Very cautiously Haki advanced. Adam led him round the sawdust ring. They made several circuits. Adam spied Mr Wiggins watching them from a front seat.

'Good!' Jake said. 'Now, if you let go the bridle, will Haki follow you?'

'Oh, yes,' Adam said confidently. 'He's been doing that since he was weaned.' He said 'Come, Haki!' Haki at once took his place with his nose almost touching Adam's shoulder. Round the ring they marched, first in one direction then another.

'Now, Adam, take this short whip. Whenever you change direction, crack it once. Haki will soon recognize it as the signal to turn.'

Adam took hold of the bridle and cracked the whip as he turned Haki smartly round. At first Haki eyed the whip, showing the whites of his eyes. When nothing unpleasant happened he began to think of the whip simply as the signal to turn. Adam kept repeating the exercise.

'Now let go the bridle again, Adam. See if Haki will turn of himself when he hears the whip crack.'

Adam walked alongside Haki, keeping the colt well to the circumference of the ring. Before long Haki knew that his place was close to the wall of the ring and he stayed there without any urging. Adam went round a couple of times, then cracked his whip. Of his own accord Haki wheeled round.

'Well, done, Haki!' Adam praised him.

'Try it again, Adam, just to make sure it wasn't a fluke,' Jake directed.

Haki went half-way round. Adam cracked his whip and Haki turned smartly.

'Good lad, Haki! He's learned it all right,' Jake shouted.

Haki knew he had done well. He nuzzled at Adam's pocket, looking for his reward of a lump of sugar. Adam turned out the lining. Luckily still one solitary cube lay there. Haki took it as his due.

'Well, Mr Wiggins?' Jake asked.

'The pony's intelligent, right enough,' Mr Wiggins looked pleased.

'Do you want him to do any more?'

'No, he's done enough for the first time. You've both shaped pretty well, Adam. All I want to see now is Adam playing his pipes and the pony marching off after him.'

Adam picked up his bagpipes, set the drones throbbing, then broke into *Scotland the Brave*. Haki followed him round the ring.

Mr Wiggins winked at Jake. 'I think I've backed a winner there.'

None of them saw Willie Baxter watching with an angry scowl.

'You wait, Scotchie!' he muttered, but the triumphant strains of *Scotland the Brave* drowned his voice.

Adam rubbed down Haki with his old towel as soon as he reached the stable. Jake came in while Adam was busy on him.

'That's a sensible lad. Always rub him down when he comes out of the ring. That's when animals catch cold, when they leave the heat of the ring for the cold night air. You both did well, Adam. I've been talking to the Boss and he thinks Haki might start by doing a short turn in the Grand Parade of the animals at the end of the show. He'll just walk in the animals' procession with you playing the pipes in front of him. That'll please the Scottish audiences, the Boss says.'

'We'll do another turn beside that, though, won't we?' Adam asked, slightly disappointed.

'Oh, yes, of course you will! But new tricks take a lot of rehearsing before you can present them to an audience. We'll start tomorrow by teaching him to rise on his hind legs when you raise your whip. I don't think he'll take long to learn that. Feed and water him now and see he's well tied up with enough length of rope so he can move round comfortably in his stall. By then I'll have the sleeping tent up for you alongside our wagon.'

Adam saw to it that Haki was quite comfortable, and left water beside him in a bucket. This time, when Adam said, 'Bye, bye, Haki, I'll be back,' Haki seemed quite reconciled to his going away. He turned, licked Adam's face, and settled down among the straw.

When Adam reached the Bradley's living wagon he found that Ella had cocoa on the stove and had made a thick pile of ham sandwiches.

'You and Haki did very well, lad,' she told him. 'I could see the Boss was right pleased.'

'Someone else was pleased to see Haki too,' Jake told her. 'Sonda! She trumpeted her call to him the way she used to call Gipsy, and what was more, Haki replied.'

'Never!'

'Aye, it's the truth!'

'Well, well!'

When supper was over Ella told Adam, 'I've made your bed up. There's a sleeping-bag and plenty of blankets. I'll give you a call in the morning at six o'clock. Your breakfast will be ready at six-thirty.'

'Thanks for everything,' Adam said, full of gratitude to his new friends. 'Good night, then.'

'Here's an electric torch. It'll help you see your way round the tent,' Jake said.

Once Adam had shut the wagon door Ella asked Jake, 'Did Bill notice the way Sonda behaved?'

'Aye, he did. I had a word with him later.'

'And what did he think about it?'

'He says it's got possibilities. He's going to let Sonda watch Haki a bit at rehearsals.'

'Good! That'll put Willie Baxter's eye out. Watch him! I don't trust that one.'

Adam thought it would be a long time before he fell asleep in this strange new world. He listened for a few minutes to the night sounds of the circus; the sudden barking of dogs that stopped at a shout from someone; the faint chattering of a monkey; the distant roar of a lion; the voices of people returning to their living-wagons. One by one the lights went out and the circus settled down to sleep. Circus folk have to rise early and hard work makes them quick to sleep. Adam closed his eyes. When he opened them again it was morning and Ella was shaking his shoulder.

The following week was one of steady rehearsal with Haki. Ella's prediction that Haki was a born trouper seemed to be fulfilled. He accepted the nearby company of other ponies and the liberty horses. In fact, he liked to watch the liberty horses at work. When they were led out he champed at his bridle and pawed the ground in impatience till Adam led him out too. He stood stock-still in the big aisle and watched all they did. He liked to watch Sonda, too, as Bill put her through her tricks. She sat down: rolled over, lay still: walked delicately among rows of upright bottles, never touching one of them, and lifted Bill on her back at the end. She began to watch for Haki at the beginning of her act and she saluted him with her trumpeting call. Haki looked at her and whinnied gently.

Then, one day Bill said something to Jake, and Jake come over to Adam and Haki.

'Bill wants to introduce Sonda to Haki. He's going to bring her over to get a nearer look at him. Do you think Haki will stand his ground all right? Sonda's a gentle, well-behaved beast and Bill says she's curious about Haki.'

'I'll hold Haki and put an arm round his neck. That always gives him confidence.'

'Right!' Jake beckoned to Bill.

Bill held on to Sonda by the curved iron pole that fitted round her leg and they advanced slowly to within a few feet of Haki. Adam held on tightly. The pony looked at Sonda in surprise.

'Steady, Haki!' Adam said quietly.

'Stand still, Sonda,' Bill commanded, pulling on the pole. Sonda obediently halted.

'Can you bring Haki a couple of paces nearer Sonda?' Bill asked. 'Stop at once if he seems inclined to back away.'

With Adam holding his bridle, Haki stepped nearer. The elephant and the Shetland pony looked at each other with interest. Haki seemed unafraid. Sonda swayed her trunk very slightly from side to side as though making up her mind about something. Then she lifted it and brushed Haki's head lightly with the tip of it. It was over almost before Adam realized what had happened.

'My goodness! She's *kissed* him!' Jake exclaimed.

'That's the old trick she used to do with Gipsy,' Bill said. 'I wonder if she'll do it again? Shall I try the old word of command?'

'Are you willing, Adam?' Jake asked. 'I don't think you've anything to fear.'

It was Haki who answered the question. He took another step forward and lifted up his head to Sonda.

Bill said, 'Go on Sonda! Give Haki a kiss!'

Sonda put out her trunk to touch Haki gently again and Haki's tongue flashed out and he licked her!

'You could knock me down with a feather!' Jake exclaimed. 'They're friends already. Sonda's taken to him. That's just grand!'

'Love at first sight!' Bill laughed. 'We'll let them have a word with each other every day. Lead Haki away now, Adam.'

As Haki was led away he gave his little whinnying cry. Sonda responded with a triumphant trumpeting call.

'Whatever made Sonda treat Haki like that?' Adam asked Jake.

'I reckon it's a kind of mother-love,' Jake said. 'When an elephant has no child of her own, she often looks round for some animal to adopt. Some elephants get fond of cats. There was a cat in one circus used to curl up every night beside her elephant friend. The only animal an elephant fears is a mouse!'

Adam laughed out loud. 'That's just absurd!'

'It's the truth,' Jake replied. 'An elephant is mortally afraid of a mouse running up inside its trunk. I'm glad Sonda's taken a fancy to Haki, though. It could lead to something.'

'To what?' Adam was mystified.

'It might lead to a turn together on the programme. That would be a real favourite with the crowds and Mr Wiggins wouldn't half be pleased. Would you be willing, Adam?'

'I might, provided there was no danger to Haki,' Adam replied cautiously.

After that, Haki watched Sonda in the ring every day. When Sonda finished her act she always looked round for Haki. Adam led him up and the two animals touched trunk and nose in friendly kiss. One day Adam held out a piece of sugar for Sonda at the same time that he gave Haki his. Sonda took it with delight. After that she always looked for her lump of sugar from Adam.

'Those two animals are half-way to being trained together,' Jake said with satisfaction.

At the end of the week Mr Wiggins thought that Haki was sufficiently rehearsed to take part in the final animal parade every night.

'We'll have to dress you up for it,' he told Adam. 'You'll need a kilt. I'll send to the theatrical costumiers in Edinburgh to let us have one or two for you to try on. We can hire one till there's time to get one made. We'll need some trappings for Haki, too, Jake. Got any in the caparison box?'

'Aye, there's a tartan saddle somewhere – Royal Stewart, I think. Perhaps we can get Adam a matching kilt.'

'I'll leave it to you to see them fitted out, Jake.'

'I'll do that, Boss.'

All that week Sonda and Haki had been rehearsing a simple turn together to Bill's great delight. Haki did his usual trick of following Adam when he played the bagpipes. This was no new thing to him but it was new to Sonda. Bill tried leading her round after Haki and Adam. At first she eyed the bagpipes dubiously. When the wail of the drones started up she looked distinctly unhappy. Then she watched Haki tripping lightly in time to the music. She watched him as he made the circuit. Then, somehow she got the message of the rhythm. First she began to sway, waving her trunk. Then, to everyone's astonishment she began to pound her feet up and down in time to the music. At once Bill led her behind Haki. The two of them went mincing along, Sonda following Haki. Haki's little hoofs hit the ground with the precision of a drummer and Sonda kept perfect time behind him with her great feet.

'Well!' Bill exclaimed. 'We could train that pair to dance.'

'You've got an idea there, Bill. Just keep Haki and Sonda at it while I fetch the Boss. He must see this.'

Mr Wiggins watched the march-round with a critical eye.

'Not bad!' he declared at the end. Jake knew that from Mr Wiggins that was high praise.

'I think Sonda should wear a bit of tartan too to connect her in the public eye with Haki. The Scottish crowds will fall for that. Any suggestions, Bill?' Mr Wiggins asked.

Bill thought for a moment. 'Didn't the circus have some long tartan curtains once?'

'Aye, they're in the property wagon,' Jake told him.

'I wonder if we could cut them lengthwise and join them up to make a big sash that would go round Sonda?'

'With a small one to go round Haki,' Jake suggested.

'They'll need some stitching of course,' Bill said, looking at Jake.

Jake took up the cue at once. 'I'll ask the missus to get her sewing-machine out right away.'

'Get on with it then,' Mr Wiggins said. 'Can you manage it for tonight?'

'Aye, Boss!' Jake said with confidence.

'It might be a good idea to let Haki and Sonda lead the parade. An honour to Scotland, you know,' Mr Wiggins said.

When the Grand Parade took place that night Adam stood ready with his bagpipes to lead it.

'Now, whatever you do, Adam, don't turn and look at Haki,' Jake cautioned him. 'Just keep marching and piping. You know he'll follow all right.'

Adam nodded. His stomach seemed to be turning over. He kept swallowing hard, wondering if he'd be able to control his breath to blow the pipes.

Mr Wiggins, in shiny black top-hat, pink hunting-coat and white riding-breeches, stood ready in the middle of the ring. He cracked his whip as a signal to start. Adam gripped the bag under his arm, started the drones and burst into *Scotland the Brave*. With his kilt swinging and the tartan ribbons flying on his bag-pipes he advanced into the ring. Mr Wiggins swung his whip to point the way for Adam to begin his circuit. With high colour and pounding heart Adam stepped out. He could hear Haki's little hoofs beating out the rhythm behind him and the stamp-stamp of Sonda's feet following. Behind Sonda came the liberty horses moving in beautiful time, with Ella riding the foremost. The other Shetland ponies drawing a cart full of chimpanzees came next, then the clowns tumbling and turning somersaults. Behind them marched the acrobats, trapezists and high-wire performers.

Adam, piping fit to bust his lungs, made two circuits of the ring, as Mr Wiggins instructed, before he led off the Parade. The applause from the audience was deafening. Haki took it all in his stride. Indeed, he looked rather pleased with himself.

Mr Wiggins said something to one of the clowns who came tumbling out of the ring. He dashed up to Bill and Adam.

'The Boss says "Can Haki and Sonda both take a bow?" If they can you're to bring them right back in the ring.'

'Sonda can bow. Can Haki?' Bill asked quickly.

'Yes. I've taught him that.'

'Come on, then! We'll have a bash! Don't bother playing your bagpipes. The band's taken up the tune.'

The other performers drew their animals to one side to let Sonda pass.

'Well done, Haki! Just fine, Adam!' came from more than one. Only one person was not pleased. Willie Baxter snarled as Adam went past. He half lifted his whip as if meaning to give Haki a cut with it.

Adam seized his wrist. 'You watch it, Willie Baxter, or I'll deal with you.' He gave Willie a push out of his way, then he led Haki proudly into the ring. Bill followed with Sonda. The applause broke out loudly again. They took the centre of the ring. Adam held out a piece of sugar to Haki and then to Sonda, on the other side of him.

'Bow, Haki!' he said, giving a deep bow himself.

At the same moment Bill said, 'Bow, Sonda!'

Haki touched the ground with his nose and Sonda went almost on to her knees.

'Now say good-night to the people, Sonda!' Bill commanded.

This was an old trick of Sonda's. She raised her trunk and trumpeted her farewell to the crowd. Hearing Sonda's voice, Haki answered.

Then, greatly daring, Bill said loudly, 'Kiss Haki good-night, Sonda.'

Sonda faced round to Haki. The tip of her trunk touched Haki's nose with great gentleness. Haki's tongue flashed out. The crowd cheered and clapped.

'And now to bed!' Bill said firmly. 'Wave to the people as you go, Sonda.' Under his breath he said to Adam, 'Lead off now, Adam.'

Adam took Haki's bridle and waved to the crowd as he made for the exit. Sonda followed, waving her trunk in the gayest fashion. The band burst into *God Save the Queen*.

Jake met them as they came out of the ring. 'Grand, lad, grand!' he said, shaking Adam by the hand. Ella was waiting in the long passage and gave Adam a hug and a kiss.

'I was right proud of you, lad!' she said.

Bill brought out Sonda. 'Well done, Adam! I guess Haki and Sonda are going to be quite a turn together.'

His heart full of joy, Adam led Haki to his stall. They had made their début in the world of the circus.

9

Friends and enemies

The circus stayed three weeks in Edinburgh, then went to Falkirk. Adam and Haki rehearsed constantly with Sonda, besides doing their short turn at the end of each programme. They were building up a longer act.

Bill introduced the *Merry Widow Waltz* into their tunes. Facing each other, Haki and Sonda were taught to rise on their hind legs and pirouette. This was no new thing to Sonda who had been doing it in her own act for some time. Haki had to learn it. Adam taught Haki to rise on his hind legs by holding his sugar high in the air at the end of a pair of tongs! Adam twirled the tongs about and Haki twisted too. By and by Haki recognized the upward gesture and the tune and rose automatically on his hind legs. He watched Sonda do her act. After that he imitated her. Soon Adam had only to lift and twirl his whip when the tune was played, to show what he wanted. The training was not done all at once. It took many weeks of patient tuition.

Haki taught Sonda a trick of his own invention. It had always been Haki's habit to push his nose into Adam's pocket to get the last lump of sugar out of the bottom. He would even seize the lining of the pocket between his teeth and pull it out to make sure the pocket *was* empty. Sonda watched Haki extract the last sugar cube several times. She thought she might as well take a turn at it herself. She edged round to Adam's other side and dipped her trunk under the flap of his pocket. Out came the last piece of sugar from *that* pocket too and with it the lining!

'Well, look at that!' Bill cried. 'Leave those animals alone and there's no knowing what mischief they'll teach each other! We must put that in the act too, Adam, so always be sure you have a last lump of sugar in the other pocket for Sonda.'

Day by day, practice by practice, the whole act was built up.

In what little spare time he had, Adam got to know most of the circus company. Most of them were friendly people who made him welcome. There were the Vivaldis, Paulo, Marco and Maria, the Italian aerialists. They swung from their trapezes like monkeys and went flashing through the air with all the grace of tropical birds. They were gay, happy folk in spite of the tremendous risks they took in the dome of the Big Top. Paulo used to play the guitar on the steps of their wagon in the evening and Marco and Maria sang Italian songs together.

There were two clowns, Auguste and Joey. Auguste was always the smart alec in the ring, taking a rise out of Joey. Joey was the pathetic one who nearly always did everything wrong, but in the end always got his own back on Auguste. Out of the Big Top, with the grease paint cleaned off, they were two handsome lads, brothers and friends.

There was Leo the lion-tamer. In the ring he held the lions in check by the power of his eye. Out of the ring he was a quiet gentle person, noted for good turns.

All these people came along to Jake's living-wagon for a cup of cocoa after the last performance. It was a brief, friendly gathering in which Adam was accepted as one of themselves. The Baxters never came near Jake's wagon, though. Usually they retired to their own quarters. The Baxters trained the chimpanzees and the two ponies that drew the cart with the monkeys driving it.

'I'll grant the Baxters are clever with the chimps,' Jake Bradley said. 'But it's just as well they don't work with the lions.'

'I don't like that chimp Cora,' Ella remarked. 'She's a sly one. She treats the other animals

badly. It's my belief Willie Baxter encourages her.'

Not long afterwards Adam went along to groom Haki ready for his performance. As he neared the stable he heard Haki whinnying with fear and clattering his feet. When Adam dashed into the stable there was Cora sitting astride Haki's back and pulling at his black mane. Haki was half mad with terror, rearing and plunging as he tried to throw her off his back.

'Get down!' Adam shouted at the monkey.

A head appeared over the top of the partition. 'Go on, Cora! Pinch him!' Willie Baxter encouraged her.

Cora needed little incitement. She pinched Haki's neck hard. He squealed with fear. He had no means of fighting back at the strange devil which tormented him. Adam had, though. He gave Cora a resounding whack on her ribs and snatched her from Haki's back. She chattered with rage and tried to claw him. Adam flung her bodily through the entrance to the stall and she fell in a heap in the passage-way.

Willie Baxter came rushing round, his fists raised.

'How dare you strike my monkey?' he yelled, livid with temper.

'Next time she touches my pony I'll take a whip to her,' Adam retorted savagely.

Cora was chattering on the ground, more angry than hurt.

'Take her away. You know she shouldn't be here at all.'

'Are you telling *me* what I ought to do, Scottie?'

'Yes. Take that monkey to her cage!'

'Look, Scottie, I've had enough of your cheek coming here and sucking up to the Boss. He let you head the Parade and I ought to have done that with the chimps. *I* ought to have had charge of that pony. I'll make you wish you'd never joined the circus!'

Adam was not prepared for Willie Baxter's rush. He had no time even to put his hands up to defend himself. Baxter landed a blow on Adam's chest which sent him staggering backwards. His very teeth jarred in his head as he fell.

'Want any more, Scottie?' Willie Baxter sneered.

Adam rose to his feet, breathing hard. When Baxter saw the black anger in Adam's face, he stepped backwards. He took a sudden run at Adam and lifted his foot to kick him. Adam was ready for him this time. He caught Baxter by the ankle and toppled him to the ground. Adam snatched a pitchfork used to fork hay into the mangers. When Baxter sat up Adam was standing in a menacing attitude.

'Get up!' Adam shouted at him. 'Get up and fasten that monkey to the pole or I'll let you have it!'

Baxter thought he meant business. He jumped to

his feet and seized the light chain that was dangling from Cora's collar. He hitched it round the post and secured it.

'Right! We don't want any interruption, do we?' Adam said grimly. 'Out into the passage now!'

The two boys faced each other in the wide, tented passage. Adam flung the pitchfork down among the hay.

'Now we'll fight fair! Put your fists up, Baxter!' he yelled.

They flew at each other, Baxter hurled himself on Adam, battering at his ribs.

Adam had done some boxing at school and he had taken part in bouts with the trawlermen at their club. He knew at once that he must keep Baxter at the length of his arm. Baxter was much heavier than he was. If he got to in-fighting Adam might get the worst of it. Adam fought him off, nipped under Baxter's fists and danced away from him. Baxter went after him savagely.

Adam stepped aside and landed a shrewd blow on the side of Baxter's head. Once again he danced lightly backwards. If Baxter had weight, Adam had speed. Again Baxter rushed at him but Adam caught him a jab in the ribs which brought him up short. Baxter began to eye Adam more warily. If only he could get close to Adam he would give him a hiding. Adam had no intention of letting Willie Baxter get in close. He darted this way and that. The blows that Willie Baxter did manage to land glanced off Adam and did little harm. Willie's breath came faster. He was not in good condition. If only he could grab hold of Adam and hold his arms to his sides. Then he might bring him to the ground. He pretended to hold back for breath but Adam did *not* rush in. He knew if Willie once got the hold of him there would be dirty fighting and he could expect no mercy.

Baxter stood hunched, glowering. 'Come on, Scottie! Are you afraid?' he panted.

Adam laughed. '*You* come to me, Baxter! Have you got no breath for any more fight?' He dropped his hands slightly.

Baxter rushed at Adam, thinking he was off his guard. Adam's fist shot out, a straight right to Baxter's nose and a short quick jab to his midriff with his left. Baxter reeled backwards. Adam followed up the attack with blows to the ribs and the chin. Baxter managed to land a blow on Adam's eye, but Adam was tough stuff. He shook his head, then hammered at his breathless adversary. Exhausted, all the fight beaten out of him, Baxter wobbled and sank to his knees.

Adam stood over him. 'Want any more, Baxter?'

Willie could only shake his head. He knew when he was beaten.

'Then listen to me,' Adam said. 'If ever you let your chimp touch my pony again, you'll get what's coming to you. You keep out of Haki's stable!'

Willie Baxter lurched to his feet. 'You wait, Scottie! I'll be even with you for this!'

At that moment Jake came along the passage

with Bill. Unbeknown to both boys they had watched the last part of the fight from the stalls of the liberty horses. Bill was for rushing in and stopping it, but Jake held him back. It was better that Adam should fight his own way at the circus. When it was plain that Willie had got the worst of it, Jake strode down the passage.

'What's going on here?' he shouted. 'Have you lads taken leave of your senses? You know the Boss doesn't allow fighting.'

Just then he almost tripped over the chain that held Cora, who was cowering behind the bale of hay.

'What's that chimp doing here?' he demanded. 'What do you mean by bringing your monkey into the stable, Baxter? You know that's against all the rules.'

Baxter looked at him sullenly.

'Why were you fighting, anyway?'

Both boys were silent; Baxter because he dare not tell that he had set the chimpanzee on to Haki; Adam from a code of conduct that would not let him be a tell-tale.

'Now, listen to me,' Jake said sternly. 'You'd better go and get cleaned up. If this comes to the Boss's ear he'll make short work of both of you. He's not over pleased with you and your ways as it is, Willie Baxter. A bonnie sight you look to go into the ring tonight! Take yourself off, and Cora too! If you bring her into the stables again, I'll tell the Boss myself.'

Baxter unhitched Cora and shambled away.

Jake turned to Adam. 'And you go see to that eye, Adam! It'll be all the colours of the rainbow by the time tonight's performance begins!'

'Please, I want to look at Haki first,' Adam begged.

'Just two minutes, then!'

The colt was still trembling slightly. Adam stroked him and talked quietly to him. 'It's all right now, Haki! It will never happen again.' The colt nuzzled at Adam and began to settle down.

When Adam reached the living-room, Ella Bradley was waiting for him with a piece of raw steak.

'Come here, Adam!' she said with pretended wrath. 'It's come to something when I've got to sacrifice today's dinner to put on your black eye, because you've been fighting! Well, did you beat him?'

'Aye!' Adam grinned as he held the steak to his eye.

'If you hadn't you'd have heard something from me,' she said.

'If Adam's got a black eye, Willie Baxter's certainly no picture,' Jake chuckled. 'He'll keep out of everyone's way for a bit.'

That night Willie did *not* lead in the chimpanzees. His brother had to stand in for him.

'What's up with Willie?' Mr Wiggins demanded.

'Had a bit of an accident. Got his face marked.

He'll be all right tomorrow,' Alec Baxter told him.

As Adam and Haki passed the chimpanzees in the Grand Parade Cora chattered angrily and Haki shied slightly away from her and fell out of step.

'Steady, Haki!' Adam said over his shoulder. 'It's all right.'

Haki resumed his jaunty march behind Adam. Sonda had noted the chattering chimpanzee and Haki's nervous movement. She was quick to connect the two. She twitched her trunk in Cora's direction and trumpeted so fiercely that she almost drowned Adam's piping. Mr Wiggins cracked his whip and the Parade went on.

When the show was over Mr Wiggins sent for Jake.

'What's going on in this circus? Nobody ever tells me anything,' he stormed. 'But I'm neither blind nor daft. One lad can't appear because his face is messed up and another lad has a swollen eye. A chimp practically swears at a lad and his pony shies, then Sonda gets mad. It all adds up to something. Now, what is it?'

'I reckon there was a bit of a fight between Willie Baxter and Adam Cromarty and Baxter didn't get the better of it,' Jake said cautiously.

'There's only one thing would rouse Adam's temper and that's trouble over his pony,' the Boss remarked shrewdly. 'How did Cora come into it? Haki didn't shy at her for nothing. Has Baxter had the chimp in the stables? Now, if he's let Cora frighten the horses, I'll not stand for it. Willie Baxter goes!'

Jake put a hand on his arm. 'Hold it, Boss! Willie Baxter's had a lesson from Adam Cromarty that he'll not forget. You'd be as well to let it go at that.'

'Well – maybe you're right, Jake. The chimps are a good turn; though it's a pity Willie has got this jealous grievance against Adam.'

'Willie thinks Adam has ousted him from his proper place in the circus.'

'He's wrong there. You can tell both lads from me, though, that if there's any more fighting I'll dock their pay for a week.'

'I'll do that, Boss,' Jake promised. 'I think it might not be a bad idea to stable Haki somewhere else. While he's stabled alongside Willie Baxter's ponies, there's always the chance of the two boys getting across with each other.'

'Where are you going to put him, then?'

'We've plenty boards and canvas. I think we could fix it next to the elephant's shelter.'

'That's a good idea, Jake. You think Sonda will watch over Haki?'

'She's terrible fond of him, sir. She wouldn't stand for any monkeying about with the pony.'

'I get you! When you say monkeying about, you mean *monkeying about*. All right! Go ahead! You can fix it with Bill and Adam.'

The very next day Haki was moved next-door to Sonda, greatly to her delight. Sonda could just look over the wooden planking between their stalls. Haki, too, seemed to find comfort in Sonda's companionship.

Willie Baxter watched these changes with disgust. 'I've not done with you yet, Scottie!' he muttered to himself.

The circus moved on to Dunfermline and Perth. In Perth it was set out on a piece of flat land near the river Tay. People flocked in to see it and the Big Top was crowded every night. Haki and Sonda, 'The Big and the Little', were tremendous favourites with the audience.

The last night of their stay in Perth Adam stabled Haki as usual next-door to Sonda. Bill tethered Sonda by a leg chain to an iron stake buried in the ground.

'Mind you, Adam, if Sonda took it into her head to uproot that stake, she could do it easily,' Bill told Adam. 'She could pull up a tree if she wanted.'

'What keeps her there, then?' Adam asked.

'Habit, I suppose. When she was a baby elephant she couldn't have pulled up the stake then, so she's got used to it. She knows it's a sign she must stay where she is. She's an obedient beast. Not much chance of her straying away, though, while she's got Haki next door. Better than a nannie to him, she is!'

Adam put out clean water for Haki and saw he had plenty of straw bedding. 'Good-night, Haki! I'll be back in the morning.' Haki nuzzled him with affection.

Adam was careful to see that the wood-and-canvas door to Haki's stable was properly secured by its bolt. Jake was always very insistent about making the animals secure, so Adam also tied two ends of rope which fastened the door to a pole.

'Good-night, Sonda!' Adam called softly as he passed Sonda's stable. Sonda replied with a friendly grunt.

That night a shadow crept up to Haki's stable and untied the rope and shot back the bolt. A moment later there was the sound of blows from a whip! Haki neighed in terror, clattered his hoofs and bolted from his stable. In a moment he had disappeared in the darkness.

'That's your hash settled!' the lad with the whip muttered. 'By morning you'll be miles away!'

Sonda was roused from sleep by Haki's frightened neighing. She poked her head outside her shelter in time to see Haki gallop away terrified from the shadowy person holding the whip. Her quick intelligence connected the lad and the whip with Haki's cry of pain. She lashed out with her trunk and snatched the whip, then dealt the man a stinging blow with it. He yelled with fear and ran for all he was worth towards the living-wagons and tents.

Sonda lunged forward to pursue him. She was brought up short by the chain on her leg. She remembered Haki. Where was he? She *must* find Haki! Sonda gave a terrific tug to her chain and stake. She pulled her hardest and the stake came out of the ground. She was free! She dashed over the meadow after Haki, dragging her chain and stake behind her, trumpeting wildly.

Sonda crashed through a low fence that Haki had leaped. She thundered across a garden, over a wall and on to the high road. She ran along the high road till she came to a lane. Again she trumpeted. Even in his headlong flight Haki heard her and slackened his speed a little. He gave his answering neigh. Sonda plunged down the lane after him.

Haki could smell the heather on the hills. The heather spelt home and safety for him. There was even a dim memory of Hecla. Between him and the hills lay the wide stretch of the fast-flowing river. Haki plunged down towards it.

Up at the circus camp Bill had been roused by Sonda's frantic trumpeting. He hitched on his trousers and ran to her shelter. It was empty! He looked in the next stable. Haki had vanished too! Bill paused only long enough to snatch up his long iron hook and a length of rope. He dashed to Jake's living-wagon and hammered on the door.

'Get up, Jake! Haki's gone and Sonda too! We've got to find them!'

Adam heard Bill's knocking and his shout. In a second he was into his trousers and pullover and had joined Bill and Jake. Haki was in danger!

'Which way did they go?' Jake demanded.

'Towards the road.'

Jake snatched up his big hand-torch. 'Come on!' he said. They set off at a run.

Jake flashed his torch along the grass of the meadow. There were marks of Sonda's feet in the soft ground. They followed them as fast as they could in the dark till they reached the broken fence.

'Sonda's certainly been here!' Bill said grimly.

A man leaned out of the bedroom window of the cottage.

'Lost something?' he asked when he saw their torch.

'Aye, an elephant!'

'It crossed my garden and made off down the road towards the river.'

'Come on, lads!' Bill cried.

'Hi! What about compensation for my fence and plants?' the man cried after them.

'See you in the morning about that! Got to catch the elephant now!' Bill shouted back.

At last they came on Sonda and Haki standing by the river brink. Sonda was standing between Haki and the water. Every movement Haki made towards the river Sonda thwarted him by her great body.

'Sonda's keeping him from the river,' Bill cried. 'Why should Haki want to go into the water?'

Adam knew, 'He'd want to cross the river to get to the hills. He could smell the heather. Any Shetland pony would take to the hills.'

'He might have been drowned,' Jake said sternly.

Adam reached Haki and put his arms around

him. The little pony trembled and nuzzled against him, nickering and whinnying.

'He's been frightened!' Adam declared.

Sonda seemed satisfied now Adam was looking after Haki. She submitted to being secured with the rope.

'How on earth did they get out?' Jake asked as they began to lead the animals back to the circus. 'Did you fasten up Haki's stable all right last night, Adam?'

'Yes, I'm sure I did,' Adam replied positively.

'I was up there taking a look at Sonda after Adam went to his tent,' Bill said. 'Haki's stable was fastened up all right then. Seeing Sonda can't untie knots, someone must have been there afterwards.'

'Looks like it,' Jake agreed. 'Someone must have let Haki loose and Sonda went after him. We all know how daft Sonda is about Haki.'

They reached the stables again. Suddenly Sonda lifted something out of her path and tossed it away from her in anger.

'What's that?' Bill asked sharply.

Jake picked it up. It was a whip!

'This looks like the cause of the trouble,' he said.

'Did someone use that on Haki?' Adam gasped, his face dark with anger. 'Whose whip is it?'

Jake examined it by his torch. 'It's a stockwhip out of the stores,' he announced. 'It could have been used by anyone in the circus. Most of us have them.'

'I'll find out who—' Adam began angrily.

Jake shook his head. 'You've no *proof*, lad. You've got to have proof before you can accuse anyone. Sonda didn't let the culprit off scot-free. A pity she can't speak! We'll all of us keep our eyes skinned. Truth has a strange way of coming out. Meanwhile you can trust Sonda to look after Haki.'

10

Fire! Fire!

The circus continued its tenting tour through the larger towns of Scotland, staying for a while in Glasgow. As summer began to wear into autumn, it headed south for Lancashire, playing to the big industrial towns.

Haki and Sonda continued to do their turn together and were great favourites. There was a wicked gleam in Sonda's eye, however, whenever she saw Willie Baxter. Willie took care to keep away from her.

Week by week Adam was saving part of his wage towards his set purpose of buying Haki back. Though they were quite happy in the circus, Adam still wanted to *own* Haki again. Of his wage of ten pounds he paid three pounds a week to Ella Bradley

142

for his food. She refused to take any more.

'Nay, lad, the tent's there to be used and the bed came from the circus stores. I wouldn't have the face to charge you for that. The money easily covers your food.'

'But there's my washing, too, and all your trouble,' Adam pointed out.

'Deary me! What's one extra in the stew-pot or the washing-tub?' Ella dismissed her generosity lightly.

Adam confided in her how he was saving up to buy Haki back.

'That's a sensible idea. But you're not thinking of leaving the circus, are you?'

'Oh, no!' Adam said hastily. 'It's just – well – Haki has always belonged to me. I send some money home to my mother every week, but I could put three pounds a week towards buying Haki. Ella, will you look after my savings for me?'

Ella hesitated. 'The money might not always be safe in the living-wagon, Adam. Jake and I have to be away from it a lot. Some queer characters come round circuses at times. You'd be better with it in the national savings bank. You could pop into a post office at every town we visited. You'd get a bit of interest on your money too.'

So every week Adam paid a visit to the post office, to send a postal order to his mother, and to put a regular sum in the savings bank. Towards the end of the circus tour his bank-book was showing a nice little credit balance.

The circus was to go into its winter quarters at a farm in Lancashire after its last show at Liverpool. Most of the animals would go to the farm, including the liberty horses, Haki and Sonda.

'The Boss says you're to go to the farm with us, Adam, and help me to look after the horses and ponies,' Jake told him during the last week.

'That's fine!' Adam exclaimed. 'I didn't want to have to be parted from any of you.'

'Least of all from Haki!' Ella teased him. 'Who is leaving the circus then, Jake?'

'The acrobats and trapezists will be going on the halls as usual, of course, but some of them will join us again in the spring. Leo's taking the Big Cats to Belle Vue Circus in Manchester, just for the winter. The Boss says he's not been over-pleased with the Baxters, so he's given them notice.'

'Thank goodness for that!' Ella exclaimed.

That night was to be the last tenting show of the season.

'There'll be no need for us to pack up tonight to be ready for the road tomorrow,' Jake said with satisfaction. 'The Boss says we can do it at our leisure. Hurrah for a good night's rest.'

'Look, Jake! Seeing we've not to be up at crack of dawn tomorrow, what about having a party for our friends tonight?'

'Suits me!' Jake said.

'Right! Pass the word round to Paulo and his troupe and Leo and the clowns, will you?' Ella said.

144

'I take it you're not inviting the Baxters?' Jake chuckled.

'I am *not*!' Ella declared.

That night Sonda and Haki gave a first-rate performance. During the last few weeks they had practised a final turn to their act. After they had said good-night to the audience Adam said to Haki, 'Come along to bed now, Haki, there's a good boy!'

Haki shook his head and stood stock still. Adam repeated the command but Haki still refused to budge. Then Adam, in pretended despair said to Sonda, 'Can *you* do anything with him, Sonda?'

Bill pointed to Haki and said, 'Up, Sonda!'

Sonda curled her trunk very gently round Haki and carried him out of the ring to the laughter and applause of the crowd.

Bill had been right. Haki had liked Sonda to stroke his back with her rippling trunk. Affection grew between them. Working slowly and patiently, Bill and Adam at last reached the 'lift and carry' stage of the act. To Sonda it came naturally. Haki had learned to trust Sonda. When, for the first time Bill said '*Up*, Sonda!' and pointed to Haki, the pony was astonished when he found himself in the air, but not alarmed.

'Down, Sonda!' Bill said at once, and Sonda set Haki gently on his feet again.

It was not till the last week of their tour that they performed this turn in public. It proved a great success.

On the last night when Adam with his bagpipes

and Haki and Sonda led the final Grand Parade, it seemed as if the audience would never let them go. Adam felt a pang of regret that it would be the last time for some months that he would lead the Parade. Not till spring would the circus go tenting again. He and Haki had indeed become part of the show.

The lights were put out in the Big Top. As Adam led Haki away to his stable Jake called after him, 'Look sharp with getting Haki bedded down, Adam. Ella wants to get the party going quickly. She wants you to help.'

'Tell Ella I'll hurry,' Adam said.

Willie Baxter heard what Jake said and glared in Adam's direction. 'So *we're* not wanted at the party! And we've got the sack from the circus! I'll fix you, Adam Cromarty, *and* your pony!' he muttered.

The party was one of the gayest the circus had ever known. Ella produced mountains of delicious food. Even the Boss looked in and was given the place of honour on the settee.

'Stand up, everybody!' Jake said. 'Lift your glasses and cups! I ask you to drink the health of Mr Wiggins, the best Boss a circus ever had! The Boss!'

'The Boss!' everyone cried with enthusiasm.

'Thanks, Jake! Thanks, all of you!' Mr. Wiggins said. 'You've been grand troupers, young and old. I hope you'll be with me at the start of the next tenting season.'

'Here's to the Circus!' Ella cried.

'The Circus!' Never was a toast drunk with more sincerity.

It was while they were drinking the second toast that the alarm came! There was a terrific trumpeting from the elephant shed. It set the lions roaring and the horses neighing and stamping. Even above the noise of the party the din could be heard.

'What's wrong with Sonda?' Bill exclaimed, opening the door of the living-wagon. 'Mercy on us! The shed's afire!'

Everyone poured out of the wagon and raced across the field. It was Haki's shed that was blazing!

'Haki! Haki!' Adam cried in horror. A terrified neighing came from the shed.

Adam got there before Bill and Jake. He wrenched open the canvas and wood door and plunged in among the smoke and flames. Even as he went in an iron pole and wooden wall collapsed, bringing the canvas roof down with it. It fell inside the stable and began to blaze.

'Haki! Haki! Where are you?' Adam stumbled round in the smoke. The heat from the fire singed his hair and eyebrows. 'Haki! Haki!' he shouted frantically.

A choked whinny answered him from the ground.

'Come out, Adam! Come out!' Jake yelled.

'Haki's pinned down by the pole and the wall!

They're wedged! I can't shift them,' Adam called desperately.

'Come out!' Jake implored him, but Adam still struggled to free Haki.

In the elephant shed Sonda was nearly going mad. She trumpeted and stamped. Bill led her out and away from the rain of sparks.

'Is Haki out?' he shouted to Jake.

'No! He's trapped. Adam won't leave him. They'll both be burned alive,' Jake cried in horror.

Bill did not hesitate. 'Come on, Sonda!' He led her up to Haki's stable. One side and the end of it were blazing furiously. The straw inside was alight too. Dimly Bill could see Adam, outlined against the flames, trying to lift the debris off Haki.

'Lift, Sonda! Lift!' Bill cried. 'Get Haki!'

Sonda often helped to lift tent poles and this was her word of command. She was shaking with fear but she heard Haki's desperate neighing. Her love for Haki was greater even than her dread of the flames. She plunged into the smoke and felt round with her trunk.

She found the pole and the wooden wall that was pinning Haki down. She thrust the blazing wooden wall aside and tugged at the pole which was wedged. It snapped off short but Haki's leg was free.

'Come on, Haki! Come on!' Adam urged, choked by the smoke. Haki struggled to rise but flopped back again. His foreleg had been broken by the falling pole.

'Up, Sonda, up!' Bill cried.

Sonda did not hesitate. Once again she thrust her trunk among the smoke and sparks and blazing straw. This time her trunk curled round Haki himself and lifted him clear of the stable. She backed away, her trunk round him, beyond the range of flying sparks. Adam stumbled from the shed, beating the fire from his clothes, in time to see Sonda place Haki gently on the ground at Bill's feet.

Haki lay there, his maimed leg doubled up, his mane and tail burnt away by the fire, but he was still alive. Adam fell on his knees beside him, forgetting his own burns.

'Oh, Haki! Haki!' he cried, the tears streaming down his face.

Jake spread blankets over Haki. 'The Boss has gone to 'phone for a vet,' he told Adam. He shook his head when he saw the sorry condition of the little animal.

'Your hands need bandaging too, Adam.'

It was only then that Adam realized that his hands had been burnt in trying to free Haki.

The rest of the company quickly ran up hoses to fight the blaze and connected them to the standpipes on the circus ground. The flames began to dwindle and die down.

The veterinary surgeon arrived quickly in his car and George Wiggins brought him to the pony. The vet gently removed the blankets and felt Haki's legs.

'The right foreleg is broken above the fetlock,' he

pronounced. 'No other bones seem to be broken but he's got several bad burns and the poor little fellow is badly shocked too. He's in a bad way.'

'Adam, maybe you'd better let the vet put him out of his misery,' Mr Wiggins said gently.

'Oh, no! No!' Adam started up. 'Not that! He *could* get well again, couldn't he?'

'Well, I could set his leg, but it will take a longish time for the bone to knit. I could dress his burns too, and give him penicillin to prevent infection. The skin would heal very slowly and he'd need almost as much nursing as a hospital patient.'

'But he *might* recover?' Adam persisted.

'With care he would. But I doubt if he'll be fit enough to take part in the circus again.'

'Better let him go, Adam. I'll get you another pony you can train,' George Wiggins offered.

'No! I don't want Haki to die!' Adam cried wildly. 'Listen, Mr Wiggins! You said I could buy back Haki any time in a year if I had fifty pounds. I'm only five pounds short. Will you take the forty-five pounds and let me pay you the rest out of my next wages?'

'There's no need for any money at all,' George Wiggins said gruffly. 'I'll *give* him back to you, Adam. Look after him if you want it that way.'

'Please can I *buy* him back?' Adam begged. 'He might not be any more use as a circus pony.'

Mr Wiggins laid a hand on Adam's shoulder. 'Let's leave it just now, Adam. We'll argue it out in a few months' time when we see how Haki goes on.

You do your best for your pony, lad. Jake and the others will help you.' Mr Wiggins blew his nose hard. He turned to the vet. 'Go ahead and make that animal as comfortable as you can and set the leg. You can send the bill to me afterwards.'

Once the leg was set and the burns dressed, Haki was lifted gently by the men into a well-lined horse-box.

'I'll stay beside him,' Adam said.

'I'll help you, Adam,' Jake said quietly. 'We'll take it in turns sleeping and watching. I've got to go along and see the Boss first, though.'

In his living-wagon George Wiggins questioned Jake. 'Have you any idea how that fire started?'

Jake hesitated, then he held out something on the palm of his hands. It was a petrol-operated cigarette lighter, charred and twisted.

'One of the lads found this just inside the stable.'

Mr Wiggins looked up sharply. 'Does Adam smoke?'

'No.'

'Do you recognize the lighter?'

'It's one of a very common pattern. There are thousands of 'em. All I can say is Willie Baxter had one like it.'

'Mm! So it looks as if the owner of that lighter set light to the hay in the stable near the wall and dropped his lighter as he scrambled out. And there's been bad blood between Willie Baxter and Adam Cromarty.'

'Willie was black-jealous of Adam.'

'Mm! We've no real *proof*, but you can send Willie Baxter to me and I'll ask him a few questions.'

'I can't do that, Boss.'

'Why not?'

'Willie Baxter and his brother and the chimps lighted out of the circus in their two wagons about the time the fire was discovered. They'll be miles away by now.'

'I'll catch up with Willie Baxter, wherever he's gone,' Mr Wiggins said determinedly. 'We'll have difficulty, though, in proving he started that fire. Now, see Adam gets all he wants for the pony. But I doubt if Haki'll ever be fit to do his turn in the Big Top again.' Mr Wiggins shook his head dolefully.

11

The show goes on

It was a long hard time for Adam and Haki in the winter quarters. Adam had a shakedown in the stable at the farm and slept alongside his pony. Every day he renewed the dressings on the colt's burned skin. He massaged Haki well where there were no burns, to keep him in condition.

At first Mr Robinson, the vet, called every day.

At the end of the week he gave Haki a careful examination.

'He'll get better. He's got a good strong heart and a hardy body. It must be all those heather shoots and sea-weed your ponies feed on when they're young,' he joked. 'But don't try to force the pace with him, boy. Nature must take her own time with healing.'

'Will he be able to walk again?' Adam asked.

'Aye, he'll walk, but I can't promise he won't be lame. Don't let him put his foot to the ground for a long time yet. It'll be time enough when he shows signs of wanting to use that leg himself.'

Every day Haki had two devoted visitors, Bill and Sonda. When Bill took Sonda out for her exercise he brought her round by Haki's stable. Every day Sonda swung out her trunk and Haki responded by licking her.

'As long as Haki remembers Sonda, there's hope he'll recover altogether,' Bill told Adam.

One day Adam called Jake into the stable. 'Look! Haki's skin has all healed except for one little patch on his flank as big as a shilling. Even that is beginning to skin over now, though it may leave a mark,' he said sadly. Adam had been so proud of Haki's shining coat.

'You'll soon be able to start grooming him again and then you can brush the hair over that patch,' Jake consoled him.

'And see, Jake! His mane and tail are growing again.'

'Bless me! So they are!' Jake declared. 'It'll take a time to grow as long and beautiful as they were before, but perhaps, by the beginning of the next tenting season, he'll be showing several inches.'

'The next tenting season?' Adam looked at Jake. 'Jake, do you think we shall see Haki under the Big Top again?'

'Adam, I can tell you it was a miracle Haki lived, burned as he was. If one miracle can happen, there's no reason why another shouldn't. Keep your faith, lad!'

At last there came a day when Mr Robinson stripped the plaster from Haki's foreleg. Adam watched him anxiously. He felt the limb all over with great care.

'The break's reunited all right,' Mr Robinson said. 'It's a good mend. The leg will be a bit stiff, though. Let him take his own time in using it. Give it a gentle massage every day.'

Adam worked on the limb very carefully. He and Haki seemed to have grown even closer friends, if that could be possible. Haki lifted his head with joy every time Adam came into the stable. Then, one day, when Adam went back to him after eating dinner at the farm-house, he found Haki standing on three legs with the injured one held in the air. To Adam's surprise Haki poked the foreleg at him with the old gesture that meant he wanted Adam to shake hands with him. Adam gave the fetlock a gentle shake, then, hardly daring to say the word aloud, he gave the command 'Down!'

Haki set the hoof neatly on the ground and when Adam said excitedly 'Stand still, Haki!' he stood four-square firmly on all four legs.

'Keep still, Haki!' Adam cried. He rushed from the stable calling 'Jake! Bill! Ella!'

They came running.

'What's wrong, Adam?' Jake panted.

'Nothing's *wrong*! Come and see Haki!'

They peered through the stable door. 'Look! He's *standing*!' Adam cried, his voice broken by joy. 'Shake hands with them, Haki!'

Haki lifted his foot to each of them in turn and 'shook hands', then set it down easily on the ground again, to everyone's joy.

'Looks like you'll be able to start training Haki again, Adam,' Jake remarked.

'I mean to!' Adam said with determination.

'Take it easily, though, son. Don't rush Haki,' Jake warned him.

'I shall take him just step by step, adding a bit of his act each day if he's able to take it,' Adam promised. 'Will you *all* help me, Bill, you and Ella, and Sonda?'

'Of course! Sonda's been pining for Haki. She'll perk up when she sees him moving round again. We shan't be able to work them together just yet, though. I've got to take Sonda for a few days to the Christmas show in Manchester.'

When Bill and Sonda did return, Bill was bubbling over with some news. At supper he told his tale.

'We met old acquaintances at the Christmas show. You'll never guess! The Baxters and the Chimps!'

'That scoundrel Willie Baxter?' Ella exclaimed.

'He didn't look overjoyed to see us and I'm sure he'll never want to clap eyes on us again,' Bill chuckled. 'Sonda saw to that!'

'Why? What happened?' the others demanded.

'We met him face to face along one of the outside paths in the park and Sonda recognized him. He turned to run but Sonda flashed out her trunk and lifted him up in the air. He let out an awful scream. I was frightened too, for fear of what Sonda might do to him.'

'What *did* she do?' Ella asked.

'She flung him away from her as hard as she could. Luckily for Willie there was a duck-pond nearby! He went into it with a mighty splash. When he came up he was smothered in mud!'

'Serve him right!' Jake said.

' "Call off your elephant! Call her off!" he yelled. Do you know it took me quite a time before I recovered my wits enough to pull Sonda away? An awful sight Willie looked, standing there in the middle of the pond plastered in mud! He had the cheek to say he'd have the law on me and my elephant.'

'And what did you say, Bill?'

'I just told him *he'd* better not mention the *law*! "There was a little matter of a fire at Wiggins'

Circus last autumn," I told him. "You never found your cigarette lighter, did you?" I tell you, he turned *yellow*. Once he got out of that pond he took to his heels like mad.'

'That's the last we'll ever hear of Willie Baxter,' Jake said.

Soon Sonda and Haki were practising together in good earnest. Haki was quickly recovering his old suppleness.

Mr Wiggins was on the Continent looking for new turns and also looking for a new pony to take Haki's place. Jake sent a telegram to Mr Wiggins, saying, 'Don't bother about new pony. Have seen one here that might suit.' He chuckled as he handed it over the post office counter.

When Mr Wiggins returned, he found the Big Top was erected in a field near the farm.

'What's the big idea of putting up the Big Top?' he asked Jake.

'Oh, Ella thought the canvas could do with patching a bit. And we've been doing some rehearsing with the animals. Some of them were a bit stiff,' Jake said, keeping a perfectly straight face. 'Oh, and I've got that Shetland pony here that I wired to you about. You can see him go through his paces tonight.'

'No hope of him being as good as Haki, I suppose,' George Wiggins said dismally.

'Do you know, I shouldn't wonder!' Jake said with a chuckle.

That night the Boss sat in state in the Big Top

while the animals were paraded before him. The strains of the bagpipes echoed down the approach alley. In strutted Adam followed by Haki placing his feet surely and lightly and Sonda following, pounding out the rhythm.

'Why! The new pony's like Haki except for his mane and tail. I wouldn't have believed it possible to train a pony in such a short time. How on earth did you manage to persuade Sonda to accept him? She was *dotty* about Haki.'

'She still is!' Jake told him. 'As for the pony's mane and tail, they're growing nicely again.'

'Why, it *is* Haki!' Mr Wiggins cried. 'I just can't believe it! Jake Bradley, I'll sack you if you pull my leg like this again!' The Boss broke into a thundering roar of laughter too. He jumped from his chair and went to join Adam in the ring.

'Well done lad! You've worked a miracle. Haki will be able to do his turn when we go tenting again.'

'Please, Mr Wiggins, can I buy Haki back now?' Adam asked. 'I've been saving all winter and I've got the money in the post office. You did promise I could buy him back again.'

Mr Wiggins looked upset. 'Aye, I know I did. But you're not thinking of leaving me and the circus yet, are you, Adam? I'd be sorry to part with you.'

'No. I still want to stay with you and the circus, Mr Wiggins. But I want Haki to belong to *me*, to be all mine.'

'I see.' Mr Wiggins wrinkled his brows. 'No, I won't sell him to you, Adam.'

'But you promised, Mr Wiggins —' Adam began.

'Wait, boy!' Mr Wiggins held up his hand. 'I won't *sell* him to you, but I'll *give* him back to you.'

'I'd rather keep my bargain,' Adam began with Shetland pride.

'I know! I know! But I'm going to make another bargain with you, Adam. If I *give* you the pony, you've to promise to stay with the Wiggins' Circus for three years.'

'But it's too generous of you, Boss,' Adam stammered.

'No, it's not. Haki was near dead but you brought him back to life. But for you there might have been no pony at all. Keep your money and your pony, Adam, but you can sign this paper to say you'll stay with me three years, in exchange for Haki.'

Adam signed, his heart full of gratitude.

'Right! Now, don't go and spend all the money you've got in the post office bank at once, lad,' the Boss advised him.

'Well, I've got a notion lined up already,' Adam said self-consciously. 'Some day I might like to have a pony herd. So I mean to buy a little Shetland mare as a wife for Haki.'

'Now isn't that strange?' Mr Wiggins replied, twinkling. 'I had a notion that we might raise our own strain of circus ponies too. But this time,

Adam, I've beaten you to it. I sent away a week ago to Ian's uncle, Mr Sinclair, to find a good little mare for me. She should be here any day now.'

'Jings! Sonda's going to have an awful busy time acting as nannie to a whole herd of ponies!' Bill laughed.

'Don't look so dumbfounded, boy!' Mr Wiggins told Adam. 'Maybe we can arrange to go into partnership over the ponies.'

'I'd like that,' Adam replied. 'I was wondering what I was going to do with the money I'd saved. I've got one thing lined up though.'

'What's that?'

'My father and mother have never been out of Shetland. I'd like to see they got a good holiday. I—I left home in a bit of a hurry, you know, Mr Wiggins.'

'And it's been on your mind, Adam?'

Adam nodded.

'Maybe they'd like to come and see what you're doing in the circus? I reckon we could fix up accommodation for them. How's that?'

'Just dandy, sir!' Adam said gratefully.